John Henry Yates

Ballads and Poems

John Henry Yates

Ballads and Poems

ISBN/EAN: 9783744786706

Printed in Europe, USA, Canada, Australia, Japan

Cover: Foto ©Andreas Hilbeck / pixelio.de

More available books at **www.hansebooks.com**

BALLADS AND POEMS

Ballads for the Old Folks
Life Lessons for the Young
Poems Humorous and Pathetic
Gospel Hymns

BY

JOHN H. YATES

CHARLES WELLS MOULTON
Buffalo, New York
1898

Inscribed

to

My life-long friend

Mrs. Adelaide Richmond Kenny.

INTRODUCTION.

M R. YATES has endeared himself to hundreds of aged people, as well as to those who love and cherish the old, by his "Ballads For The Old Folks" which have appeared from time to time, fragmentarily, in the public prints. Rarely do poems so faithfully represent the moods and meditations of the aged as these of Mr. Yates have done. The soulfulness of his poems have moved many a heart, and moistened many an eye; their incisiveness has impaled many an error and left it quivering and dying. He has by the exercise of his poetic gift brought comfort to the sorrowing and rebuke to the impious. He has put into the mouths of the aged touching regrets for the wanton obliteration of old landmarks by the progressive, rushing, civilization of these modern times; and yet, not one of his characters is caught repining; they rather acquiesce cheerfully in the improvements of the day. One aged man goes to church —the model church—where everything is changed. A tear steals down his cheek as a swift rush of memories recall the past with its plain meeting house and simple services, but the old man forgets all this when the polite usher attentively shows him to one of the best pews where he sits joyfully, as the old tunes are sung and the Gospel is preached in its purity, as in the days of his youth. Mr. Yates' poems have had a wide circulation. Like beautiful autumn-tinted leaves, they have been wafted by the gales of popular favor hither and thither, and I, for one, am glad that they are gathered up at last, and substantially bound together in this garland. The author still resides in Batavia, N. Y., where he was born November 21st, 1837.

JOHN WENTWORTH SANBORN.

CONTENTS.

HYMNS.

BALLADS.

WELL, wife, I've found the model church! I
worshiped there today!
It made me think of good old times before my
hair was gray.
The meetin' house was finer, far, than they
were years ago,
But then I felt, when I went in, it wasn't built for show.

The sexton didn't seat me away back by the door;
He knew that I was old and deaf, as well as old and poor;
He must have been a Christian, for he led me slowly
through
The long isle of that crowded church to find a pleasant
pew.

I wish you'd heard the singing; it had the old-time ring;
The preacher said, with trumpet voice, "Let all the peo-
ple sing"!
The tune was Coronation, and the music upward rolled,
'Till I thought I heard the angels striking all their harps
of gold.

My deafness seemed to melt away: my spirit caught the
fire;
I joined my feeble, tremblin' voice with that melodious
choir,
And sang, as in my youthful days "Let angels prostrate
fall;
Bring forth the royal diadem and crown Him Lord of all."

(1)

I tell you, wife, it did me good to sing that hymn once
    more;
I felt like some wrecked mariner who gets a glimpse of
    shore;
I almost wanted to lay down this weather-beaten form,
And anchor in the blessed port, forever from the storm.

The preachin'? Well, I can't just tell all that the
    preacher said;
I know it wasn't written; I know it wasn't read;
He hadn't time to read it, for the lightnin' of his eye
Went flashing 'long from pew to pew, nor passed a sin-
    ner by.

The sermon wasn't flowery, 'twas simple gospel truth;
It fitted poor old men like me; it fitted hopeful youth.
'Twas full of consolation for weary hearts that bleed;
'Twas full of invitations to Christ, and not to creed.

The preacher made sin hideous in Gentiles and in Jews;
He shot the golden sentences down on the finest pews,
And—though I can't see very well—I saw the falling tear
That told me Hell was some ways off, and Heaven very
    near.

How swift those golden moments fled within that holy
    place!
How brightly beamed the light of Heaven from every
    happy face!
Again I longed for that sweet time when friend shall
    meet with friend
Where congregations ne'er break up, and Sabbaths have
    no end.

I hope to meet that minister—that congregation, too—
In the dear home beyond the stars that shine from
    heaven's blue;
I doubt not I'll remember, beyond life's evening, gray,
The happy hour of worship in that model church today.

Dear wife, the fight will soon be fought—the victory be
    won;
The shinin' goal is just ahead; the race is nearly run.
O'er the river we are nearin' they are throngin' to the shore
To shout our safe arrival where the weary weep no more.

✿

THE STYLISH CHURCH.

WELL, wife, I've been to church today—been to
    a Stylish one—
    And seein' you can't go from home I'll tell you
    what was done;
    You would have been surprised to see what I
    saw there today;
The sisters were fixed up so fine they hardly bowed to pray.

I had on these coarse clothes of mine—not much the
    worse for wear—
But, then, they knew I wasn't one they call a millionaire;
They led the old man to a seat a few steps from the door;
'Twas bookless, and uncushioned,—a reserved seat for
    the poor.

Pretty soon in came a stranger with gold ring and cloth-
    ing fine,
They took him to a cushioned pew far in advance of mine;

I thought that wan't exactly right, to seat him up so near,
When he was young, and I was old, and very hard to hear.

But, then, there's no accountin' for what some people do;
The finest clothin', now-a-days, oft gets the finest pew;
But when we reach the blessed home,—all undefiled by
    sin—
We'll see wealth beggin' at the gate, while poverty
    goes in.

I couldn't hear the sermon, I sat so far away,
So, through the hour of service, I could only "watch
    and pray";
Watch the doin's of the Christians settin' near me, 'round
    about;
Pray that God would make them pure within as they
    were pure without.

While I set there lookin' all around upon the gay and
    great;
I kept thinkin' of the rich man and the beggar at his gate;
How, by all but dogs forsaken, the poor beggar's form
    grew cold,
And the angels bore his spirit to the mansions built of
    gold.

How at last the rich man perished and his spirit took its
    flight
From the purple and fine linen to the home of endless
    night;
There he learned as he stood gazin' at the beggar in the
    sky,
"It isn't all of life to live nor all of death to die."

I doubt not there were wealthy sires in that religious fold
Who went up from their dwellings like the Pharisee of old;
Then returned home from their worship, with a head up-
    lifted high,
To spurn the hungry from their door with naught to
    satisfy.

Out, out, with such professions; they are doin' more to-
    day
To stop the weary sinner from the gospel's shinin' way
Than all the books of infidels; than all that has been tried
Since Christ was born in Bethelem—since Christ was
    crucified.

How simple are the works of God, and yet how very grand;
The shells in ocean caverns, the flowers on the land;
He gilds the clouds of evenin' with the gold-light from
    His throne,
Not for the rich man only, not for the poor alone.

Then why should man look down on man, because of
    lack of gold ?
Why seat him in the poorest pew because his clothes are
    old ?
A heart with noble motives, a heart that God has blest,
May be beatin' Heaven's music 'neath a faded coat and
    vest.

I'm old—I may be childish—but I love simplicity;
I love to see it shinin' in a Christian's piety;
Jesus told us in His sermons, in Judea's mountains wild,
He that wants to go to Heaven must be like a little child.

Our heads are growin' gray, dear wife—our hearts are
    beatin' slow—
In a little while the Master will call for us to go;
When we reach the pearly gateway, and look in with joy-
    ful eyes,
We'll see no stylish worship in the temple of the skies.

*

THE NEW CHURCH.

THEY'VE left the old church, Nancy, and gone
    into a new;
    There's paintings on the windows, and cushions in
      each pew;
    I looked up at the shepherd, then around upon
      the sheep,
And thought what great inducements for the drowsy
    one's to sleep.

Yes! When I saw the cushions, and the flowers fine and
    gay,
In all the sisters' bonnets, I couldn't help but say:
"Must I be carried to the skies on flowery beds of ease,
While others fought to win the prize, and sailed through
    bloody seas"?

The peacher read the good old hymn sung in our youth-
    ful days—
"Oh for a thousand tongues to sing my great Redeem-
    er's praise"!

And, though a thousand tongues were there, they didn't
    catch the fire,
And so the good old hymn was sung by a new-fangled
    choir.

I doubt not but the people called the music very fine,
But if they heard a word they said, they've better ears
    than mine,
For the new tune in the new church was a very twisting
    thing,
And not much like the tunes of old that Christians used
    to sing.

Why, Nancy, in the good old times the singing sounded
    more
Like the noise of many waters as they beat upon the shore;
For everybody knew the tunes, and everybody sang,
And the churches, though not quite so fine, with hallelu-
    jahs rang.

I'm not a real old fogy, but I sometimes want to scold,
When I see our people leave good ways simply because
    they're old;
I've served the Lord nigh forty years, and 'til I'm 'neath
    the sod,
I shall always love the simple, good old ways of serving
    God.

"The Lord's ear is not heavy," he can hear a sinner's cry,
In a church that is not painted like a rainbow in the sky;
"The Lord's arm is not shortened," He will save a sin-
    ner, now,
Though he may, in lonely hovel, on a cold earth-altar
    bow.

But they've left the old church, Nancy, and gone into a
    new,
And I fear they've gone in more for style than for the
    good and true;
And from the talk I overheard I fear that, sadder yet,
In beating other churches they've got deeply into debt.

We didn't think of lotteries and grab bags, years ago
As means of raising money to make a better show;
When Zion needed money we all with one accord,
Put our hands down in our pockets and gave it to the
    Lord.

While I was at the meetin', lookin' 'round from pew to
    pew,
I saw no familiar faces for the faces all were new;
When the services were ended all the members passed
    me by;
None were there to greet the old man with gray hairs
    and failing eye.

Then I knew that God had taken to His temple in the
    skies
All the soldiers that with you and I fought hard to win
    the prize;
I some doubt if Christians now-a-days will reach the
    streets of gold
Any better in the new ways than they did in the old.

For the Lord looks not on tinsel; His spirit will depart
When the love of world grandeur takes possession of the
    heart;

The Lord of life and glory will pass through a hovel door
Sooner than through temple portals where are no seats
for the poor.

In a little while, dear Nancy, we will lay our armor down
And from the King Eternal we'll receive a starry crown;
Then we'll meet the saintly pilgrims that we worshiped
with of old,
And we'll worship there, together, in the city built of
gold.

GOING WEST TO DIE.

WELL, here we are, my dear old wife, on board
the train at last!
Our little all packed in a trunk, with lock and
straps made fast,
I hear the bell a ringin', and the whistle's
piercin' cry;
There, wife, we're movin' out of town! we're goin' west
to die!

We've been from Jane's to John's house, from John's
house back to Jane,
Till, now, they've laid their burdens down on board this
western train;
Tis rather hard to send us off, all crippled up and gray,
To find a place in which to die, two thousand miles away.

Since we broke up a keepin' house, they've carted us
around,
Till, now, it seems, a home for us on earth cannot be
found;

As sure as this old face of mine can ne'er look young
    again,
So sure we'll never more return to trouble John or Jane.

They send us to a stranger-land, o'er an untraveled road,
That Mary in her western home, may bear the heavy load;
It isn't to be wondered at that my eyes fill with tears,
Or that my form is bendin' with more than weight of
    years.

I did n't think 'twould come to this—I didn't mean it
    should—
No home is like your own home, tho' made of logs of
    wood;
No bread is sweet when eating it 'mid bitterness and
    strife;
Few care to fill with peace and joy an old man's closing
    life.

Now, o'er a long, untraveled road we seek a stranger
    land—
The old home circle broken up at cruel time's command;
But time cannot destroy our love, 'tis stronger now than
    when
Our heads wore not the silver locks of three score years
    and ten.

Since we broke up a keepin' house we've led a wretched
    life;
Jane puts the blame upon her man, and John upon his
    wife;
They think not of their infancy—of all those tender years
When we toiled day and night for them, and wiped their
    flowin' tears.

We leave behind us all the scenes of early years, dear wife;
And all the friends with whom we've won the victories of
life;
We leave behind the little church, where oft we've knelt
in prayer,
But, good wife, we will never leave the God that met us
there.

Although these eyes are growin' dim, I still can see to
read
The precious truths in God's own Word, that children
all should heed:
"Honor thy father," saith the Lord,—"thy mother
honor too:
"Then shalt thou live long in the land that God hath
given you."

Our latest day will dawn ere long—our journey's end is
nigh—
We're goin' west to Mary's home, we're goin' west to die;
Then He who sees the sparrow fall, who counts the ocean's
sands,
Will take us to the better home—the house not made
with hands.

❧

THE OLD WAYS AND THE NEW.

I'VE just come in from the meadow, wife, where the
grass is tall and green;
I hobbled out upon my cane to see John's new
machine:

It made my old eyes snap again to see that mower mow,
And I heaved a sigh for the scythe I swung some twenty
years ago.

Many and many 's the day I've mowed 'neath the rays of
the scorching sun,
Till I thought my poor old back would break ere my task
for the day was done;
I often think of the days of toil in the fields all over the
farm,
Till I feel the sweat on my wrinkled brow, and the old
pain come in my arm.

It was hard work, it was slow work, a-swinging the old
scythe then;
Unlike the mower that went through the grass like death
through the ranks of men:
I stood and looked 'til my old eyes ached, amazed at its
speed and power:
The work that it took me a day to do it done in one short
hour.

John said that I hadn't seen the half; when he goes to
cuttin' his wheat,
I shall see him reap it and rake it and bind it in bundles neat;
And soon a Yankee will come along and set to work and
larn
To reap it, and thresh it, and bag it up, and send it into
the barn.

John kinder laughed when he said it, but I said to the
hired men,
I have seen so much on my pilgrimage through my three
score years and ten,

That I wouldn't be surprised to see a railroad in the air,
Or a Yankee in a flyin' ship a-goin' most anywhere.

There's a difference in the work I done, and the work my
    boys now do;
Steady and slow in the old-time way, worry and fret in
    the new:
But somehow I think there was happiness crowded into
    those toiling days,
That the fast young men of the present will not see till
    they change their ways.

To think that I ever should live to see work done in this
    wonderful way,
Old tools are of little service now, and farmin' is almost
    play;
The women have got their sewin'-machines, their wring-
    ers, and every sich thing,
And now play croquet in the door yard, or sit in the
    parlor and sing.

'Twasn't you that had it so easy, wife, in the days so long
    gone by;
You riz up airly, and sat up late, a-toilin' for you and I.
There were cows to milk; there was butter to make; and
    many a day did you stand
A-washin' my toil-stained garments, and ringin' 'em out
    by hand.

Ah! wife, our children will never see the hard work we
    have seen,
For the heavy task, and the long task is now done with a
    machine;

No longer the noise of the scythe I hear, the mower—
  there! hear it afar?
A-rattlin' along through the tall stout grass with the
  noise of a railroad car.

Well, the old tools now are shoved away; they stand
  a-gatherin' rust,
Like many an old man I have seen put aside with only a
  crust;
When the eye grows dim, when the step is weak, when
  the strength goes out of his arm,
The best thing a poor old man can do is to hold the deed
  of the farm.

There is one old way that they can't improve, although it
  has been tried,
By men who have studied, and studied, and worried till
  they died:
It has shone undimmed for ages like gold refined from its
  dross,
It's the way to the kingdom of heaven, by the simple
  way of the cross.

※

JOHN'S GONE OFF TODAY.

IT'S come about! I feared it would; yes, John's gone
  off to-day,
And left me alone on a mortgaged farm, without any
  means to pay—
  Gone off with the very woman who has hated me for
    years—
Who has planted my path with thorns while I watered
  them with my tears.

Perhaps 'tis foolish to mourn; perhaps 'tis better so;
When love goes out of the dwelling the loveless man
    should go.
But the heart can't let go quickly from the one it has
    loved so long
Though suddenly comes the tempest, though terrible be
    the wrong.

I gave him my youthful love in the far home over the sea;
Through all the years of our wedded life his heart has
    been true to me
Till this woman came to our table, with her fine sheep's
    clothing on,
To prove but a wolf, as she has to-day, by running away
    with John.

It is hard to work, as I have worked, for love and a home
    when old,
Then find I have garnered nothing but fond hopes dead
    and cold;
It is hard to love, as I have loved, then hear the old
    neighbors say,
John wouldn't have done this wrong but I scolded him
    night and day.

There isn't the proof in scripture that Adam was drove
    to sin;
There isn't a wife around here more patient than I have
    been;
A woman's tongue may drive a man out of the house for
    awhile,_
But to lead him astray from wisdom's way there's noth-
    ing like her smile.

'Twas the smile of this evil woman, 'twas the honeyed
    words of her tongue,
That shattered love's golden bowl, and love's tuneful
    harp unstrung;
When the serpent's charm is broken, and John comes
    back to his mind
He will sigh again for the true love of the heart he has
    left behind.

Will I run to the door to meet him?　Will I welcome him
    home with a kiss?
Supposing I do it, neighbor, will that be doing amiss?
Its dangerous sailing without the man who has been at
    the helm so long,
And they who are prone to evil should learn to forgive a
    wrong.

I often take my Bible, the well-worn one on the stand,
And read of the prodigal son coming home from the
    famine land;
Didn't the father run to meet him?　Didn't he kiss his
    repenting boy
And order a fatted calf killed to make him a feast of joy?

So will I welcome John, when his wayward race is run;
Is not a prodigal husband as good as a prodigal son?
If I forgive his trespasses, obeying the law divine,
The Lord who pities the erring will surely pardon mine.

It will come about, it will; Yes, John will come home
    soon;
Together we'll mend love's broken bowl, love's unstrung
    harp we'll tune;

Then the fatted calf I'll kill, and the news I'll spread
    around—
My John, though dead, is alive again, though lost, he
    now is found.

        *

THE FAST MAIL AND THE STAGE.

AY by the weekly, Betsey; it's old, like you
    and I;
  And read the morning's daily, with its pages
    scarcely dry,
    While you and I were sleepin', they were printing
      them to-day,
In the city by the ocean, several hundred miles away.

"How'd I get it?" Bless you Betsey, you needn't doubt
    and laugh.
It didn't drop down from the clouds, nor come by tele-
    graph;
I got it by the lightning mail we've read about, you
    know—
The mail that Jonathan got up about a month ago.

We farmers livin' 'round the hill went to the town to-day
To see the fast mail catch the bags that hung beside the
    way;
Quick as a flash from thunder clouds, whose tempest
    sweep the sky
The bags were caught on board the train as it went
    roarin' by.

We are seein' many changes in our fast declinin' years;
Strange rumors now are soundin' in our hard-of-hearin'
   cars.
Ere the sleep that knows no wakin' comes to waft us
   o'er the stream
Some great power may be takin' all the self-conceit from
   steam.

Well do we remember, Betsey, when the postman carried
   mails,
Ridin' horseback through the forest 'long the lonely Indian trails;
How impatiently we waited—we were earnest lovers
   then—
For our letters comin' slowly, many miles, thro' wood
   and glen.

Many times, you know, we missed them—for the postman never came—
Then, not knowing what had happened, we did each the
   other blame;
Long those lover quarrels lasted, but the God who melts
   the proud
Brought our strayin' hearts together, and let sunshine
   through the cloud.

Then, at last, the tidings reached us that the faithful
   postman fell
Before the forest savage, with his wild terrific yell;
And your letters lay and mouldered, while the sweet birds
   sang above
And I was sayin' bitter things about a woman's love.

Long and tedious were the journeys—few and far between
    the mails
In the days when we were courtin'—when we thrashed
    with wooden flails;
Now the white winged cars are flyin' 'long the shores of
    inland seas,
And younger lovers read their notes 'mid luxury and ease.

We have witnessed many changes in our three-score years
    and ten:
We no longer sit and wonder at discoveries of men;
In the shadow of life's evenin' we rejoice that our boys
Are not called to meet the hardships that embittered half
    our joys.

Like the old mail through the forest, youthful years go
    slowly by;
Like the fast mail of the present, manhood's years how
    swift they fly;
We are sitting in the shadows; soon shall break life's
    brittle cord,
Soon shall come the welcome summons by the fast mail
    of the Lord.

THE OLD MAN IN THE PALACE CAR.

WELL, Betsey, this beats everything our eyes
    have ever seen!
We're ridin' in a palace fit for any king or
    queen.

We didn't go as fast as this nor on such cushions
    rest,
When we left New England years ago to seek a home
    out West.

We rode through this same country, but not as we now
    ride—
You sat within a stage-coach, while I trudged on by your
    side;
Instead of ridin' on a rail, I carried one, you know
To pry the old coach from the mire through which we
    had to go.

Let's see: that's fifty years ago—just arter we were wed;
Your eyes were then like diamonds bright, your cheeks
    like roses red;
Now, Betsey, people call us old, and push us off one side,
Just as they have the old slow coach in which we used to
    ride.

I wonder if young married folks to-day would condescend
To take a weddin'-tour like ours, with log-house at the
    end?
Much of the sentimental love that sets young cheeks
    aglow
Would die to meet the hardships of fifty years ago.

Our love grew stronger as we toiled; though food and
    clothes were coarse,
None ever saw us in the courts a-huntin' a divorce;
Love leveled down the mountains and made low places
    high;
Love sang a song to cheer us when clouds and storms
    were nigh.

I'm glad to see the world move on, to hear the engine's
    roar,
And all about the cables stretchin' now from shore to
    shore;
Our mission is accomplished, with toil we both are
    through;
The Lord just lets us live awhile to see how young folks
    do.

Whew, Betsey, how we're flyin'! See the farms and towns
    go by!
It makes my gray hair stand on end; it dims my failin'
    eye.
Soon we'll be through our journey, and in the house so
    good
That stands within a dozen rods of where the log one
    stood.

How slow—like old-time coaches—our youthful years
    went by!
The years when we were livin' 'neath a bright New Eng-
    land sky:
Swifter than palace cars now fly our later years have
    flown,
Till now we journey hand in hand down to the grave
    alone.

I can hear the whistle blowin' on life's fast-flyin' train;
Only a few more stations in the valley now remain.
Soon we'll reach the home eternal, with its glories all
    untold,
And stop at the blest station in the city built of gold.

TO THE GRAVE THROUGH THE POOR-HOUSE GATE.

"Cursed be he that setteth light by his father or his mother. And all the people shall say amen."—Bible.

FUNERAL here to-day? Not much of a funeral sir!
When an old man dies in the poor-house it doesn't make much of a stir.
There's a corpse in there in a coffin with silvery hairs for a crown;
There's a vacant chair by the window; there's a load lifted off from the town.

To the grave through this poor-house gate an old man goes to-day,
And his son a wealthy farmer, but two or three miles away;
He died of a broken heart—"of age" they say, I expect—
And his wife is failing day by day through a cruel son's neglect.

Methinks the angels of God from the sinless land will come
To meet the pilgrim of eighty on the way to his narrow home.
Perhaps o'er his grave they'll bow, in their shining white array,
For no mourners of Earth will weep at the pauper's grave today.

Stranger! I'm looking rough—but the rough are often
    true—
While I'm talking about my friend you must pardon a
    tear or two.
I've known the old man long; I've talked with him much,
    of late,
When he hobbled out in the sun to lean on the poor-
    house gate.

This heartless boy of his hadn't even a garret-room
To offer the poor old folks, 'till death should offer the
    tomb;
Not a crust of bread gave he from his acres of bursting sod;
If there isn't a hell for such a man, why then there isn't
    a God!

When the sowers go forth to sow, this miser sows his grain,
And the windows of heaven open to give the refreshing
    rain;
When the reapers go forth to reap, his heavy wheat bows
    down
As his poor old father bowed to the charity of the town.

The mercy of God is great; the justice of God is sure;
Man may, but He will never forsake the feeble and poor.
Whatsoever we sow we reap. If we make others harvest
    tears,
We may look for a weeping time when we bow with the
    burden of years.

This miser son has sons; they are growing saucy and strong;
We are hurrying thro' the years; the moments may roll
    along

When he who despised his father, for the Angel of Death
    shall wait,
Looking out thro' the poor-house window, and down by
    the poor-house gate.

I'd like to be the keeper, when he is a pauper, there;
Each day I'd stop and ask him, as he sat, alone, in his
    chair,
How do you like the cup you to your father gave?
How do you like the poor-house?—how would you like
    the grave?

In the Bible I've seen it written, "With what measure ye
    mete to men
The same—be it good, or evil—shall be measured to you
    again,"
When his retribution cometh, may God round the meas-
    ure well!
If the good taste, here, of heaven, why shouldn't he of hell?

To the grave through the poor-house gate!—hush!
    hush! the corpse goes by!
Somehow! I feel in my heart there are angel bearers
    nigh:
Move on, God's burial band!; lay the silvery hairs away!
For no mourners of Earth will weep at the pauper's grave
    today.

There, stranger, the last sad act for the poor old man is
    done!
The load is off the town, now, a curse is on the son,
Another traveler has gone—where so many sad ones go—
To the better home above, from the poor-house home
    below.

THE WIFE THAT HE BROUGHT FROM TOWN.

VERY fine day for the auction, Sir! An' there's
    quite a crowd out too;
Guess things will sell for a good round price, as
    the most of 'em are new;
    I don't mind seein' a few old traps sold off at
      the hammer's blow,
But 'twill kinder make my heart ache, sir, to see the old
    farm go.

You look like a stranger in these parts! Have you come
    up here to buy?
A Yankee must ask questions, sir, if he don't he'll surely
    die:
Would you like to know the reason why this fine farm
    must be sold?
Well, sit down here and I'll tell again the tale I've so
    often told.

You see I've known Charley Jones for years—in fact,
    ever since he was born;
When a little shaver he used to come to help in my field
    of corn;
I took to likin' the young chap then, as he sat a huskin'
    the ears,
An' the friendship formed in the old cornfield grew strong
    with the passin' years.

"'Twasn't drinkin', nor gamin', nor any sich thing, that
    brought Charley down to this:
He slakes his thirst at the old farm-spring that the wild
    flowers stoop to kiss:
The only gamin' that Charley does—or has, from his
    childhood, done—
Is a huntin' the squrrels, down in the wood, with his
    faithful dog and gun.

His good old mother—now dead and gone—brought him
    up in the way he should go;
She pictured out, as a mother can, the broad road that
    leads to woe;
Charley often says, as he struggles hard, 'neath the heavy
    load of his cares,
That his hands would drop, and his heart give up, but
    for thoughts of his mother's prayers.

The truth is, stranger,—and those who know, have a long
    time marked it down—
The loss of the farm is the fault of the wife that he
    brought up here from town;
Her studied ways, and her winnin' smiles, flung around
    his heart a charm;
He married her for her pretty face, and she married him
    for the farm.

She soon grew tired of a farmer's life; the smiles were
    put off for a frown:
She sighed for the ball and the concert room; for the
    bustle and show of the town;

Charley still loved her, with a patient love; he humored
    her every whim,
Though something kept whisperin' in his ears that she
    loved pleasure more than him.

Thus things went on for a year or two; each month his
    affairs grew worse;
To supply her real and imagined wants drew heavy on
    Charley's purse:
At last, when he came from his work one night, long
    after the sun was down,
She declared, with a stamp of her pretty foot, he must
    buy her a house in town.

So a house he bought, on a pleasant street, and fitted it
    up to a charm:
But to pay for his village paradise he must mortgage the
    dear old farm:
Now, stranger, you know that the city folks are all nearly
    taxed to death:
They are taxed for the street, for the light for their feet,
    they are almost taxed for their breath.

Charley found this out in a very short time—his heart
    was filled with alarm:
For with taxes, and interest, and keepin' up style, he
    saw he must lose the farm:
When he spoke about sellin' the house in town his wife
    firmly answered "No!"
The mortgage is due; his money is gone; and now the
    old farm must go.

Some women are preachin' about their rights an raisin'
    a hul-la-ba-loo!
This woman of Charley's gets her's, I think, and most
    of her husband's too;
Charley knows two things he has dearly learned; that a
    woman's will is strong,
And that runnin' in debt to keep up style is a poor way
    of gettin' along.

So, you see, 'twasn't drinkin' nor any sich thing that
    brought Charley down to this;
He will miss his drink from the old farm-spring that the
    wild flowers stoop to kiss;
I hate to see him a walkin' around the farm with his head
    cast down;
An' I hate worse than pizen that wife of his that he
    brought up here from town.

WHAT RUINED FARMER BROWN.

WELL, wife, the end has come at last! Old
    farmer Brown is dead!
The neighbors found him in his house, stretched
    cold and stiff in bed:
Beneath the rags that covered him, held firm in
    a death hug,
They found, with every drop drained out, his old brown
    whiskey jug.

How sad to live a life like his; how sad like him to die
Alone in a deserted house, no friends or kindred nigh!

To stagger down from manhood to the gloomy river's
    brink,
The happiness of earth and heaven a sacrifice to drink.

And what was farmer Brown, dear wife, a few short
    years ago!
An honest, toiling, sober man; kind to both friend and
    foe;
There was no better farm than his in all this neighbor-
    hood;
Well fenced, well watered and well tilled; the barns and
    houses good.

His wife was happy and content,—singing from morn till
    night,
For everything upon the farm and in the house went
    right,
Until the tempter came, and said, "You have much
    goods in store,
Now eat and drink, rich farmer Brown let toiling days
    be o'er."

He listened to the tempter, and that was his great sin;
He hired men to sow the seed and reap the harvest in;
He left off following the plow; he gave all work a frown,
And hitching up his finest horse drove often to the town.

Men put him up for office, and learned him all the tricks
That constitute a scholar in the school of politics;
This brought him often to the bar to drink with all the
    ring,
And another strong Goliah fell—a victim to the sling.

From that date things went downward as by a whirl-
    wind's arm,
And Brown was soon a drunkard upon a ruined farm;
The fences down; a leaky house; no crops to gather in,
No grain in store for future wants in spacious barn and bin.

One cold and dreary autumn, when the leaves were fall-
    ing down,
His wife died, broken hearted, and was buried by the
    town;
'Tis well there is an after life, made up of perfect bliss
For broken-hearted, weary wives, who find no joy in this.

And now the end has come at last, as it doth surely come
To all who bind upon themselves the cruel chains of rum;
He left his work to others, for the bar room in the town,
And that, dear wife, was surely what ruined farmer
    Brown.

                 *

A MOTHER'S WARNING.

THERE! John, hitch Dobbin to the post; come
    near me and sit down;
    Your mother wants to talk to you before you
    drive to town;
    My hairs are gray, I soon shall rest within the
    silent grave;
Not long will mother pilot you o'er life's tempestuous
    wave.

I've watched o'er you from infancy till now you are a man,
And I have always loved you as a mother only can;

At morning, and at evening, I have prayed the God of
    love
To bless and guide my darling boy to the bright home
    above.

A mother's eye is searching, John, old age can't dim its
    sight
When watching o'er an only child to see if he does right;
And very lately I have seen what has aroused my fears,
And made my pillows hard at night and moistened it
    with tears.

I've seen a light within your eye, upon your cheeks a
    glow,
That told me you are in the road that leads to shame and
    woe:
Oh! John, don't turn away your head and on my coun
    sel frown,
Stay more upon the dear old farm; there's danger in the
    town.

Remember what the poet says—long years have proved it
    true—
That "Satin finds some mischief still for idle hands to do";
If you live on in idleness, with those who love the bowl,
You'll dig yourself a drunkard's grave, and wreck your
    deathless soul.

Your father, John, is growing old; his days are nearly
    through;
Oh! He has labored very hard to save the farm for you;
But it will go to ruin, soon, and poverty will frown,
If you keep hitching Dobbin up to drive into the town.

Your prospects for the future are very bright, my son:
Not many have your start in life when they are twenty-
    one;
Your star that shines so brightly now, in darkness will
    decline
If you forget your mother's words and tarry at the wine.

Turn back, my boy, now, in your youth; stay by the
    dear old farm;
The Lord of Hosts will save you with His powerful right
    arm.
Not long will mother pilot you o'er life's tempestuous
    wave,
Then light her pathway with your love down to the silent
    grave.

THE FORTY-ACRE FARM.

I 'M thinkin', wife, of neighbor Jones, that man of stal-
    wart arm—
He lives in peace and plenty on a forty-acre farm,
While men are all around us, with hands and hearts
    asore,
Who own two hundred acres, and still are wantin' more.

His is a pretty little farm—a pretty little house;
He has a lovin' wife within, as quiet as a mouse:
His children play around the door—their father's life to
    charm,
Lookin' as neat and tidy as the tidy little farm.

No weeds are in the cornfields; no thistles in the oats;
His horses show good keepin' by their fine and glossy
    coats;

The cows within the meadow, restin' 'neath the beechen
    shade
Learn all their gentle manners from the gentle milking
    maid.

Within the fields—on Saturday—he leaves no cradled
    grain
To be gathered in on Sunday for fear of comin' rain;
He makes that day a day of rest; his children learn his
    ways,
And plenty fills his barn and bin after the harvest days,

He never has a lawsuit, to take him to the town,
For the very simple reason, there are no line-fences down;
The bar-room in the village does not have for him a
    charm;
I can always find my neighbor on his forty-acre farm.

His acres are so very few he plows them very deep:
'Tis his own hands that turn the sod—'tis his own hands
    that reap;
He has a place for everything, and things are in their
    place:
The sunshine rests upon his fields—contentment on his
    face.

May we not learn a lesson, wife, from prudent neighbor
    Jones,
And not— for what we haven't got—give vent to sighs
    and moans;
The rich arn't always happy, nor free from life's alarms,
But blest are they who live content, though small may
    be their farms

THE TICKLISH SCHOOL OF LAW.

"WE are never too old to learn," they say; and,
    wife, I think 'tis true,
For, old as I am, I have learned today what
    before I never knew;
It is this: that to play with lawyers is the
    costliest of sports;
That 'tis better to suffer an injury than to take it to the
    courts.

We have got a stubborn neighbor; he's as mean as he is
    rich;
He needs to be taught a lesson more than most boys
    need a switch:
So I undertook to teach him, at the ticklish school of law,
And we both got scratched with the long, sharp nails
    that are hid in the lion's paw.

You know that from morn till evening, and from evening
    until morn,
His cattle are either in my wheat or in my field of corn;
In vain I have put the fences up—a work it was his to
    do—
The cattle were so unruly they still kept breaking
    through.

Well! I reckoned up the damage that they did in one
    short day,
And showed it to a lawyer, and he said "Make him pay!"

So I put the job into his hands, and told him to do his
    best;
And, wife, I really think he did, too—feather his own
    fine nest.

When the day for trial came around I thought that my
    foe would beat,
But the jury gave me just enough to pay for my ruined
    wheat;
Then the lawyer on the other side, to secure a larger fee,
Carried it up to a higher court, and there they van-
    quished me.

Now what is the use of lawin', and chasin' the town
    about?
One court will knit up justice and another ravel it out;
This playing with law and lawyers is the costliest of
    sports;
It is cheaper to suffer injury than to take it to the courts.

My neighbor found this lesson true, when he footed his
    lawyer's bill,
For I saw him shaking his head and fist as he came home
    over the hill;
He had his pockets well run through with a lawyer's fine-
    tooth comb;
'Twould have been better for him to have paid for the
    wheat, and for me to have stayed at home.

Now, wife, I will try a different plan this troublesome foe
    to rout;
A plan that will fix his fences up and keep his cattle out;

I will do him all the good I can; in doing so I'll prove
What virtue there is in the gospel law, the beautiful law of
   love.

It will not be long till he and I are sleeping beneath the
   sod;
In the little time that I have to live I will try the law of
   God;
It will take some grace to do it, for it reads like this, I
   think :
"If thine enemy hunger, feed him; if he thirst, then give
   him drink."

NO TOLLING BELL TODAY.

THEY would not open the church today, nor toll
      the solemn bell;
   Sad and short were the services at the home he
      loved so well:
   They closed the coffin and read awhile from the
      book he loved to search,
Then bore him away from a holy home, if not from a
   stylish church.

For three-score years he served the Lord until his head
   was gray;
For three-score years he blest the world with good deeds,
   day by day;
Then when his reason forsook the throne that tottered
   beneath his years,
His own hand severed the brittle thread that bound to
   this vale of tears.

For this—the act of a clouded mind, and not a sinful
heart—
The holy brethren closed their eyes and solemnly stood
apart;
For this the soldier of the cross was quietly laid away,
And the bell in the stylish temple's tower refused to toll
today.

Like the smoke from Jewish altars did the old man's
prayers arise,
At morning and at evening, to the God of earth and
skies;
Like the good Samaritan of old, the poor he gladly fed,
And only a prayer was his reward when he lay in his
coffin—dead.

Oh! Why will men with a heavy creed on bigotry's high-
way plod,
With greater love for religious forms than for a righteous
God ?
Oh! When will the sun of a better day shine down from
the skies above,
When Christians shall see with clearer eyes and love with
a broader love ?

A church with carpeted aisles, and dim, by worshipers
softly trod,
May be a house for repeating prayers, and yet not a
house of God;
A pillow of stones at midnight hour, in desert or wilderness,
May be the city's pearly gate where angels wait to bless.

The God who rules on high, though great, is ever a God
of love;
The earth cannot contain Him, nor the limitless space
above;
He may be found at altar grand, beneath the temple's
dome,
Or by the lowly cottager within his peaceful home.

They would not open the church today—where the old
man oft had been—
But the Lord threw open the pearly gates and welcomed
the pilgrim in;
They would not toll the bell today—on the way to the
grave, so cold—
But the angels welcomed the old man home with music
from harps of gold.

✤

THE OLD MAN GOES TO SCHOOL.

I KNOW I'm too old to learn, wife, my lessons and
tasks are done,
The dews of Life's evenin' glisten in the light of
Life's settin' sun,
To the grave by the side of my fathers, they'll carry
me soon away;
But I wanted to see how the world has grown, so I hobbled
to school today.

I couldn't atold 'twas a school-house; it towered up to
the skies;
I gazed on the noble structure, till dimmer grew these
old eyes.

My thoughts went back to the log-house—the school-
house of years ago—
Where I studied and romped with the merry boys who
sleep where the daisies grow.

I was startled out of my dreamin' by the tones of its
monster bell,
On these ears that are growin' deaf, the sweet notes rose
and fell;
I entered the massive door, and sat in the proffered
chair,
An old man wrinkled and gray, in the midst of the
young and fair.

Like a garden of bloomin' roses, the school-room appeared to me—
The children were all so tidy—their faces so full of
glee,
They stared at me when I entered, then broke o'er the
wisperin' rule,
And said with a smile to each other "the old man's a
comin' to school."

When the country, here, was new, wife—when I was a
scholar-lad—
Our readin', writin' and spellin' were 'bout all the studies
we had.
We cleared up the farm through the summer, then traveled through woods and snow,
To the log-house in the openin'—the school-house of
years ago.

Now, boys go to school in a palace, and study hard Latin,
    and Greek;
They are taught to write scholarly essays; they are drilled
    on the stage to speak;
They go into the district hopper, but come out through
    the college spout;
And this is the way the schools of our land are grindin'
    our great men out.

Let 'em grind! let 'em grind, dear wife! the world
    needs the good and true;
Let the children out of the old house, and trot 'em into
    the new,
I'll cheerfully pay my taxes, and say to this age of mind,
All aboard! all aboard! go ahead! if you leave the old
    man behind.

Our system of common schools is the nation's glory and
    crown;
May the arm be palsied ever, that is lifted to tear it,
    down;
If bigot's cannot endure the light of our glowin' skies,
Let them go to oppression's shores, where Liberty bleeds
    and dies.

I'm glad I have been today to the new house, large and
    grand;
With pride I think of my toils in this liberty-lovin' land;
I've seen a palace arise, where the old log school-house
    stood,
And gardens of beauty bloom, where the shadows fell in
    the wood.

To the grave by the side of my fathers, they'll carry me
    soon, away;
Then I'll go to a higher school than the one I have seen
    today;
Where the Master of masters teacheth—where the scholars
    never grow old—
From glory to glory I'll graduate in the beautiful col-
    lege of gold.

THE OLD MAN'S RETROSPECT.

A PRIZE BALLAD.

WE'VE had a meetin' Nancy, we gray-haired
    pioneers—
    We talked about, and sang about the things
    of other years;
    It sot my brain a-thinkin', and I am a-thinkin'
    still,
How fast the world advances, thro' man's inventive skill.

This don't look like the country we came to, years ago;
And where are the good people that then we used to
    know?
The graveyard mounds are many, on yonder little hill,
And hearts that beat in sympathy are now forever still.

The change has been so gradual,—we've seen it with our
    eyes,
Or I should think an angel had tuck us to the skies
While we were sleepin', Nancy, and put us down again
Upon another planet, to live with other men.

We came here in an ox-team; we scarce could see the sky,
The thickets were so tangled, the forests were so high;
Now, yonder in the valley, the palace cars fly past,
Like arrows of the hunter, like leaves before the blast.

We cleared a little corner, with sharp axe and with fire,
And roses soon were bloomin' beside the native briar;
With logs we built our cabin; we were as happy there,
As in this larger dwelling, that needs the greater care.

I miss the dear old fireplace—the back log blazin' high,
When bitter blasts of winter are sweepin' thro' the sky;
I miss the children's voices, that made me happy then;
The girls have grown to women, the boys to stalwart men,

While dozin' in my rocker, I seem to see, again,
The golden pumpkin stewin' while hangin' on the crane,
I see the iron candlestick—the snuffers on the tray;
The spinnin' wheel, and ancient clock, the marvel of its
        day.

I see you with your needles, a-knittin' by the fire,
Or busy with your distaff, as though you'd never tire;
I hear your plaintive lullaby, while rockin' John and
        Jane,
Within the rustic cradle we ne'er shall see again.

Though I am old, dear Nancy, I'd like once more to see,
And join the noisy frolic of the merry huskin' bee.
I got the "red ear" often, from many a pretty girl,
Because I slily stole a kiss, or pulled an auburn curl.

Then came the apple parin', round hearth-stones warm
and bright,
Where, with our songs and stories, we lingered half the
night,
The lassies, with long parin's, and cheeks as red as
flame,
Would toss them o'er their shoulders, to spell their
lover's name.

Ah! Those were days of happiness, as well as days of toil;
At eve we drove our cares away, by day we tilled the soil:
The innocent amusements of fifty years ago,
Gave girls and boys the sparklin' eye, and set their
cheeks aglow.

Where are the tools of pioneers—the cradle, scythe, and
flail?
To do the work of this fast age, like you and I, they fail:
The reaper sweeps the harvest fields, the mower cuts the
lawn,
And like the ways of other days, we too, will soon be gone.

Where is the postman, Nancy, with the New England
mail?
How slow he was a comin', along the Indian trail;
And some poor fellows never came—in solitude they fell,
Before the savage tomahawk, with none the tale to tell.

Now, everywhere, o er all the earth, the latest news is
known
By the far reachin' telegraph, and speakin' telephone;
And fast trains gather up the mails, along the iron path,
As whirlwinds do the autumn leaves that fall before
their wrath.

The pleasure rides of girls and boys, in olden times, were
  rare,
For roads were, mostly, corduroy, and stumps were every-
  where;
Now, mounted on their bicycles and tricycles, they glide
As noiseless as a summer cloud, or sail-boat on the tide.

Look at the churches, Nancy, with cushioned walnut
  pews,
And windows gaily painted in all the rainbow's hues;
When we first met to worship, with neighbors 'bout a
  score,
We reverently knelt to pray, upon the great barn floor.

No organs then; with tunin' fork, I started every tune;
Old "Arlington," and "Ortonville," "Dundee," and
  "Bonny Doon;"
Ah, those were days of singin', and they are tunes to
  sing:
With one accord, we praised the Lord, and made the
  rafters ring.

The swallows twittered overhead, and peeped out from
  each nest,
Kept by the same dear Father, that gave us peace and
  rest;
Within that place of worship, so rough, but clean and
  neat,
The Lord came down, our bliss to crown, around the
  mercy seat.

Well, well, what next, dear Nancy ? What will our children see,
If men keep on inventin', throughout the years to be ?

The world is growin' wiser; can't say—I wish I could—
That keeping pace with wisdom, the world is growin'
    good.

There is a better country, our feet have never trod;
There, everything is perfect—the workmanship of God:
We almost catch the breezes of that celestial land;
We almost hear its music, so near the gates we stand.

⚜

THE FARMER'S GOLDEN WEDDING.

'TIS fifty years ago, dear wife, just fifty years to-
    day
Since we hitched up together to tread life's weary
    way.
The recollections of that time are with me yet,
    you see,
When you said "no" to other lads and answered "yes"
    to me.

What troubles have we waded through, what pleasures
    have we seen,
Since I was one-and-twenty, wife, and you were sweet
    eighteen;
The winter hills are white without, our heads are like
    the snow,
And not so rosy are our cheeks as they were years ago.

What though no guests are here tonight to greet us now
    we're old?
What though we sip no ruby wine from goblets made of
    gold?

We've got the water from the spring that has not ceased
    to flow,
I like the old love that made us one just fifty years ago.

The spring is 'bout the only thing that looks as it did
    then,
For time writes many changes on farms as well as men;
But, then, there is this difference—I know and do not
    guess—
Time makes a well-worked farm worth more—a well-
    worked farmer less.

Where are the woods that stood between your father's
    farm and our's
Where oft we wandered in our youth to gather wild-wood
    flowers?
There's only here and there a tree, left towering to the
    sky,
And they are scarred by lightning strokes, and scarred
    are you and I.

And where are our companions who frolicked with us so,
Around the district school-house, just fifty years ago.
Their names are written on the stones that head the
    mounds of earth
And none are left to chat with us around our cheerful
    hearth.

Through all these years of joys and tears how kind the
    Lord has been,—
How helpful when we've gone astray, forgiving every sin!
Now we are looking forward to the city made of gold,
And though the years of youth are fled, we feel we are
    not old;

For has not Christ, in that dear book, to every mortal
    said
That he that will believe in Him shall live though he
    were dead?
And he that liveth, and believes in Him, shall never die,
But reign forever in the home that knows no dimming
    eye?

Why look then back on youthful days? Why mourn
    for pleasures fled?
Let us beneath our silver locks in patience look ahead;
For o'er the vale of shadows, in the city built of gold,
They'll cease to measure life by years, they'll cease to
    call us old.

JOHN! TURN THE OLD MARE OUT TO GRASS.

JOHN! turn the old mare out to grass, where it is
    tall and sweet;
But, first, knock off the well worn shoes that now
    are on her feet;
    No more we'll drive her on the road, or hitch her
        to the plow,
She's been a faithful beast for years, we'll feed and rest
    her now.

I bought her many years ago, before you, John, could
    talk;
She gave you your first horse-back ride upon a gentle
    walk;
Mother and I walked by her side and held you on her
    back,
As quietly she moved along the beaten meadow track.

Mother has gone and left us, John, she's at the home
    above,
Sitting within the circle, at the great feast of love;
You know before her weary feet had touched the river's
    swell,
She wanted us, for her dear sake, to use old Nancy well.

I've driv' the old mare many miles; she never ran away,
She never skeered at anything she saw, by night or day.
She's done some tall work, that I know, in smooth and
    stony places
And no one ever knew her yet to kick outside the traces.

She's seen the day that she could trot with any of the
    nags;
About her beauty and her speed I've often made my
    brags;
But she is old and stiffened now, she must feel some as I;
I can't do what I used to could before my youth went by;

She's earned the best grass in the field, the best oats in
    the barn
And she shall have them while 'tis I that runs this 'ere
    consarn;
When you are one-and-twenty, John, I'll give the farm
    to you,
Then you must do with Nancy as you see your father do.

Some men are cruel in their hearts, they love to use the
    goad,
Old worn-out horses, and old men, they turn them out to
    road;

Don't follow in their footsteps, John, who walk the road
    to hell,
But when you come to work the farm, use me and Nancy
    well.

There! turn the old mare out to grass, where it is tall
    and sweet,
She must feel better now, I think, those shoes are off her
    feet:
Put her within the meadow, that has the flowing spring,
For she is old, and she shall have the best of everything.

$*$

BLUE GLASS AND TELEPHONES.

HURRAH for blue glass, Nancy! Hurrah for tele-
    phones!
    I'll get the aches and pains drawn out of these
    old, crippled bones
      And then I'll tell our children—our John and
      Mary Jane,
Who, went away so long ago on board that western train.

I'll tell them—I'll not write it, my old hands tremble
    so—
Nor will I telegraph it, that's old style, now, you know;
I'll telephone it all the way, then they can sit and hear
The poor old voice they haven't heard in many a weary
    year.

What am I crazy over, now? What do I talk about?
Why, Nancy, read the papers more, and let your knittin'
    out,

Then you will know what's goin' on in this inventive land;
No longer, now, are our old ways so wonderful and
grand.

They say they have diskivered that blue glass cures the
Gout
And puts Neuralgia, Rheumatis, and other aches to rout;
You sit and let the sun's warm rays shine on you through
the blue,
Then, leaving all the old behind, you get up young
and new.

Why, blue glass makes the flowers bloom and larger,
stronger grow;
It makes the farmer's sickly lambs stand up and skippin'
go;
They say 'twill make the maidens more rosy and more
bright
As they wait for their lovers upon a Sunday night.

If this is so, then to my mind, it clearly doth explain
Why Yankees go ahead so fast and such great honors
gain;
Behold our starry banner! See its corner large and blue!
Say, don't the sun's rays shine through that, down on
their hearts so true?

Well, what about the telephones? That's harder to ex-
plain;
You sit within the little room and talk, or sing a strain,
And men a thousand miles away can hear the word, and
tune,
And tell you what you're singing, good old "Mear" or
"Bonny Doon."

Hurrah for blue glass physic!   Hurrah for telephones!
I'll get the aches and pains drawn out of these old crip-
    pled bones
Then I will tell the story, that John and Jane may hear
The tremblin' voice they haven't heard in many a weary
    year.

Well, well, there's one far City inventions cannot reach;
No voice can ever come from there, no matter what men
    teach;
Nor will the sainted ones we love appear to glad our eyes
Until we go to meet them in the glory of the skies.

No telegraphs or telephones can reach the saints in light,
To take the sounds from this poor world still wrapped
    in error's night;
The curses, and the wails of woe from hearts by anguish
    riven
Would mar—would utterly destroy the harmony of
    heaven.

THEIR DOLLARS AND DIMES WOULDN'T WED.

WELL, Nancy, our neighbors have parted, with
        terrible words and a frown;
    John's wife and her things are all carted away to
        a house in the town;
    This time they have quarreled for certain—this
        time they have parted for life;
For Jane won't go back to her husband, and John won't
    run after his wife.

"When a woman says won't, it is ended," the truth of
    the saying is plain;
So the matter will never be mended, for John is as stub-
    born as Jane.
How foolish to toil on together, then part at the set of
    the sun—
To balk and kick over the traces when all of the pullin'
    is done.

It wasn't a new quarrel, Nancy, but a very old family
    bone,
Over which they contended together, over which they
    have brooded, alone;
This constant contendin' and broodin' has parted love's
    cable in twain,
And these hearts fly away from each other, alone to meet
    trouble and pain.

Why didn't they find it out sooner that they couldn't to-
    gether agree?
Well, well, Nancy, sure I can't tell you! The thing is a
    mystery to me;
If, when they were young, they had parted, instead of
    dwelling in strife,
Then Jane might have had a new husband, and John
    might have got a new wife.

If love is the light of a dwelling, a man can put up with
    a crust;
Sometimes we bear things for we love to—sometimes we
    bear things for we must;

Some people are happy when fighting—uneasy and rest-
    less they'd be,
Like a cat in a garret of strangers, if a moment of peace
    they should see.

Why didn't they fight awhile longer, after having con-
    tended so long?
That preachers may tell you in sermons—that poets may
    sing you in song;
I know that a ship that keeps leakin' may ride through
    the storm o'er the crest
And go down within sight of the harbor, where the winds
    and the waves are at rest.

A breath from the lips of the mornin' will put out the
    flickerin' light
Of a lamp that is never replenished, tho' brightly it shone
    on the night.
And this is the how and the wherefore this parting has
    been brought about;
They never replenished their love-lamp and now it's for-
    ever gone out.

They made a mistake when they married; the preacher
    the service said o'er,
But, somehow, he wasn't successful in joining together
    their store:
It didn't take long, I can tell you, to get the truth into
    the head
That though hands were coupled together, their dollars
    and cents wouldn't wed.

The time came when John must have money—to whom
  will man go in this life
For a friend to assist him in trouble, if he hasn't a
  friend in his wife?
To the wife that could help him he hasted, and quickly
  he hasted away—
He staid 'bout as long with his banker as a man near to
  hornets will stay.

Then off to the brokers John bolted—with face very
  black with a frown,—
To the men who go up in the balance by the weight of
  the men who go down:
To the brokers he went for his money, and a nice little
  shave did he pay,
And the weight of that burden I reckon weighs down the
  poor fellow today.

And this was the wife that he married! Far happier
  John would have been
Had he taken a wife from the poorhouse to save her
  from hunger and sin;
Though hands, and though hearts are united, if dollars
  and dimes are apart,
The demon of selfishness surely will ruin the hopes of the
  heart.

Well, Jane still hangs on to her money—she lives with it
  now in the town,
Alone she gets up in the morning, alone she at night
  lieth down;

I fear that the idol she worships, for which through these
    years she has striven,
In cheating her out of her earth-home will finally cheat
    her of heaven.

Well, Nancy there isn't much danger that we for such
    reasons will part!
We haven't gone much to the bankers our treasures are
    locked in the heart;
And we're wearin' the priceless treasure that shall weigh
    every other down,
A home with the King Eternal and a never fadin' crown.

THE TWO PRAYERS.

'GOD bless the poor!" the rich man said
    As by the fire he sat and read
    The tales of woe—the hopes destroyed—
    Among the thousands unemployed:
"God bless the poor through this cold wave!"
He prayed, and prayed, but—nothing gave.

"God bless the poor!" the widow sighed
As she her needles deftly plied,
Knitting the stockings, warm and strong,
Singing a glad thanksgiving song;
And when the stockings were complete
She drew them on the chilly feet
Of ragged urchins from the street.

Tell me, ye scholars of the cross,
Which prayer was gold and which was dross.

THE FARMER'S CHRISTMAS EVE.

FETCH up a little sweet cider, John: and wife,
　　bring the doughnuts out!
　For the winds of a dreary winter are blowin' fiercely
　　about;
　The work of the summer is ended and here are the
　　winter snows;
I have earned the roof that shelters us all, and the right
to toast my toes.

Well! Another year has rolled around, and Christmas
eve is here;
Take down the Bible, Mary—your eyes are young and
　clear,—
And read about the shepherds, how the angels came to
　them
And told them the great Christ was born in lowly Beth-
　lehem.

Somehow it soundeth sweeter when read at Christmas
　eve;
As sweeter sound God's promises to those who mourn
　and grieve;
Who knows but holy angels look down on us tonight,
Although we hear no "peace on earth," although we see
　no light?

Somehow, I cannot help it, I feel my boy is there
Among the angels, looking down upon his vacant chair;

Somehow, I cannot help it, I try my thoughts to check,
I feel his face against my cheek, his arms around my
neck.

There, wife, brush off those starting tears! Our angel
boy, tonight
Enjoys a brighter Christmas eve among the saints in
light;
We shall not hear his voice below, we ne'er shall speak to
him,
But we shall see him, by-and-by, with eyes no longer dim.

I see you've found the place, my child, so I'll be still
and smoke
While you read about the chorus that all Bethlehem
awoke

      *   *   *   *   *   *   *   *

While you were reading, Mary, about the Saviour's birth,
Although I did not hear the song, I felt the "peace on
earth"
And should the heavenly choir e'er come down to earth
again,
I'd join my feeble voice with theirs, and sing "good
will to men."

Ah! Got the stockings all hung up along the kitchen
wall ?
You think, no doubt, that Santa Claus will give our home
a call;
Well, shouldn't wonder if he did! He's rather odd, you
know,
And loves to please the children, though his path lies
through the snow.

Now I've been thinkin' all the while that I've been
    smokin' here
That if God gives us such good gifts, and fills our home
    with cheer,
We ought to do for others; the Book says, I believe
"It is more blessed, far, to give, than it is to receive."

So, John, get up tomorrow, at the earliest mornin' beam
And hitch up Bob and Jimmy, our strongest workin'
    team;
Then get a load of body wood, and provisions, on the
    sleigh,
And take them to the little cot of afflicted widow Gray.

For what's the good of wishing that the poor were
    warmed and fed
And not give the wood to warm them, and withhold the
    loaves of bread?
If all Christians would, with noble deeds their life of
    faith adorn
There'd be happiness among the poor each merry Christ-
    mas morn.

LONGING FOR THE OLD HOME.

A BALLAD OF THE WEST.

IT'S thirty years ago, dear wife—they called us "old
    folks" then —
Since we left our far Eastern home, to toil with West-
    ern men;
    Oft as I sit beside the fire, and watch the embers glow,
I long, once more, to see the home we left so long ago.

The great Creator made the heart with tendrils to entwine
Around old scenes, as to the oak clings fast the ivy-vine;
They say that sea-shells sing of shore, where break the
    waves in spray,
So sings my soul of dear old friends, and old scenes far
    away.

· The sun at even tints the clouds, and fringes them with
    gold,
Thus memory glorifies our youth when we are worn and
    old;
Then blame me not if I look back and brood o'er van-
    ished joys,
Or laugh again at tricks I've played on other roguish
    boys.

The more I think about it, wife, the more I think I'll go,
Although I'm old and feeble, now, with hair as white as
    snow;
I long to see the dear old home so many miles away;
I long to see the dear old friends, like us grown old and
    gray.

So pack my trunk tomorrow, wife, with the few things
    I'll need,
And on the lightning train bound East away from here
    I'll speed;
At eve the girls can play for you, and sing some cheery
    strain,
And soon the lightning train bound West, will whirl me
    home again.

I'll die a little easier —when comes my time to die—
If, once again, those sunlit spires dawn on my fading
    eye;
I'll start off more contented to the bright, eternal land
If, once again, the friends of old may press my withered
    hand.

Only talking?   Only dreaming?   Don't you think I
    mean to go?
Well, I know I've harped upon it, as I've watched the
    embers glow,
But this time I am in earnest, so then, Betsey, face
    about!
Lay your paper by a moment, while I plan my visit out.

First of all I'll seek the old home where I passed my boy-
    hood days,
And the worn old oaken bucket to my trembling lips I'll
    raise :
Then I'll step inside the cottage, with a feebler tread, I
    know,
Than when last I crossed the threshold on that day so
    long ago.

What pleasure it will be to me to take another smoke
Where I've heard the crickets singing, and have laughed
    o'er many a joke;
There I'll listen to the roaring of the logs that upward
    blaze,
Until I fall asleep and dream of boyhood's sunny days.

When darker shadows 'round the hearth proclaim the
    close of day,
I'll kneel, where, with our little ones, we'e often knelt
    to pray;
There, years ago, my mother bowed beside the old arm
    chair,
And taught my infant lips to say the Lord's, sweet, holy
    prayer.

What deep impressions can be made upon the youthful
    mind—
Impressions that shine bright and clear when years are
    left behind;
While the effect of sermons preached to men grown old
    and proud,
Is not as lasting as the tints of sunset on the cloud.

A mother's prayers to God to keep her child from sin
    and crime,—
Like letters chiseled in the rock—defy the waves of Time;
Though, for awhile, the boy forgets, he feels, in after
    years,
The drawing of her tender words—the pleading of her
    tears.

But I'm digressing from my theme—I'm straying from
    my text;
After I've seen the dear old home, where will I visit next?
The neighbors? Yes, yes, every one for miles around
    I'll see,
And tell the old tales o'er again, and laugh right merrily.

Then when the Sabbath morning dawns, and skies are
    all aglow,
With some old friend, to the old church with faltering
    steps I'll go,
Once more to hear the truths of God from dear old
    Parson Steele—
Once more within the old, old pew, his eloquence to feel.

The old stone church, I recollect—yes, in the days of
    yore,
A deacon found a snake coiled up before the very door,
And would-be prophets shook their heads, and said with
    visage sad,
"This church, so full of prayer and praise will end in
    something bad."

There, Betsey, I will plan no more—It's bed time, now,
    I know;
I shouldn't wonder if in dreams to the old home I'll go.
But dreaming will not satisfy the longing of my heart,
So pack my trunk tomorrow, wife, and Eastward I'll
    depart.

      *   *   *   *   *   *   *   *

Take off the strappings, Betsey! The old brown trunk
    unpack!
To the old Eastern village I'll never more go back;
I know you'll call me silly—you'll say my mind doth
    roam;
Take off the strappings, Betsey, I've got no other home!

Today I met a stranger selling goods of Eastern make
In the store where I was trading—where a frequent
    smoke I take,
One by one he showed his samples, talking as he laid
    them down,
And I overheard him saying he was from my native town.

Then my heart did warm up tow'rd him, and I drew him
    to the fire,
And asked a thousand questions—guess I did the
    stranger tire—
Then the answers that he gave me, and the things he
    told me there,
Tore away the fairy castles I had builded in the air.

The quiet little village we left many years ago
Is a busy, growing city, with a constant ebb and flow;
All the buildings we remember have been swept by fire
    away,
And great blocks of brick and granite kiss the very
    clouds today.

The old stone church has ended as the prophets prophe-
    sied,
For a grog-shop now is in it, with the snake coiled up
    inside;
Few are living, 'mong the Christians, who with us did
    watch and pray,
All the rest are sleeping sweetly 'neath the tombstones
    cold and gray.

And the Parson—dear old soldier—sleeps beside the flock
  he led,
While the breezes of the summer moan above the silent
  dead;
Thus our comrades in old conflicts sleep where daisies
  catch the dews,
And unholy hands have broken down the pulpit and the
  pews.

The old home? 'Tis rebuilded in the style of modern
  days,
With no fireplace for the crickets—where the logs can
  roar and blaze;
And the inmates are so stylish they do never laugh and
  joke,
So, of course, they've got no corner where a poor old
  man can smoke.

Guess I must be growing childish; it seems so very
  strange
That I forgot we're living in a world of death and change;
But stronger men than I am—and wiser men by far
Think of things just as they wish them, not of things
  just as they are.

In our memories, brightly shining, live the home and
  friends of old,
Soon the voice of Death will call us to the mansions
  built of gold;
When our glad eyes gaze upon them with one heart and
  voice we'll sing,
"Oh! Grave, where is thy victory? Oh! Death, where
  is thy sting?"

WHEN MY OLD HAT WAS NEW.

DON'T laugh at my old hat, dear wife, 'tis much
like you and **I**,
Although I've got a better one, I'm loth to lay
it by;
While sitting by a cheerful fire its signs of wear I
view,
And think how swift have flown the days since my old
hat was new.

While sitting by my cheerful fire some other thoughts
arise,
Suggested by the poor old hat that hangs before my eyes;
I think how many friends I had that time has proved
untrue;
What loud professions they did make—when my old hat
was new.

I read of fraud on every hand—where thieves high office
hold—
I read how, on election days, men's votes are bought and
sold;
This land will go to ruin soon, if ruled by such a crew;
An honest man was king of men when my old hat was
new.

Now, when man slays his fellow-man, they raise this
flimsy plea—
"Done in the act of self-defence" or "in insanity;"

Then to a parlor-cell he goes to stay a day or two;
They hung such men, and did it well, when my old hat
was new.

In many of our churches, now, the rich, alone, bow
down;
The poor are in the by-ways and hovels of the town.
I think—if I remember right—the poor, the wealthy too,
Met, brother-like, to worship God, when my old hat was
new.

As the nation groweth richer, men of pomp and pride increase;
As the nation groweth stronger, shouts for war disturb
the peace;
Better go a little slower—for the slow way is the true—
Then we'll grow as we've been growin' since my old hat
was new.

*

MARRIED AGAIN AT SEVENTY.

MARRIED again at seventy? Isn't that rather
old
To set his affections on things below, so nigh the
city of gold?
So nigh the valley of shadows, where wives and
husbands part?
Well, Love is a funny fellow, to shoot at an old man's
heart.

'Twill set the women talking; by some it will be said
The poor old man is foolish thus in old age to wed.

But young folks say light things, because they do not know
What it is to be left alone when the head is white as snow.

I saw the old man lately; I met him on the street;
I thought that he was looking uncommon prim and neat;
'Tis strange he did not tell me, that I might wish him joy,
For he was chipper as a girl, and laughing like a boy.

The Bible says, "It is not good for man to be alone;"
The influence of woman gives to life a better tone.
If this applied to Adam, in Eden's sunny bowers,
Why shouldn't to an old man amid the withering flowers?

I'm glad the old man's married; I'm glad his wife is old;
The silver hairs have crowded out the flowing locks of gold.
Together, now, they'll journey beneath life's evenin' sky;
Together, likely, they'll lay down their burdens by and by.

'Tis better thus, I'm thinking—the old the old to wed—
Than for a girl to marry a man with silver head.
When maidens marry old men, nine times in ten you'll find
'Tis for the houses and the lands the old men leave behind.

I'm glad the old man's married, tho' very great his age—
He'll add to life's bright record another shining page;
His children all have left him for firesides of their own,
And o'er his first companion's grave the grasses long have grown.

I've seen two streams united near-by the ocean's shore:
They ran on smooth together 'till they joined the billows,
    roar,
May not two lives, uniting, flow on undimmed by tears,
Tho' first they come together near the ending of their
    years?

Then send the old men courting. Yes, let the old men
    wed!
Tho' form be bent and head be gray, the heart may not
    be dead.
If woman's love and sympathy our earthly Eden makes,
'Tis good to have when life's sweet lyre its saddast music
    wakes.

THE OLD TRAMP'S STORY.

THANK you kind policeman, for a bed upon the
    floor!
    It wasn't soft, like some I've had in happy
    days long past,
  Excuse an old man's tears, for those days can come
    no more,
And death will send this pauper, soon, beyond the
    winter's blast.

Will you hear an old man's story, who must soon pass
    from your sight
  To continue his long journey—a wreck upon the wave?
My sun of life is sinkin'; I am entering the night
  That is followed by a mornin' in the lands beyond the
    grave.

Are you weary hearin' stories that you hardly can believe?
　Are you weary seein' beggars, comin' in from out the
　　cold ?
Don't let your heart get hardened; for the angels stop
　to grieve
　When they see the helpless misery of thousands poor
　　and old.

Once I had a happy home, sir—on a bright, New Eng-
　land shore—
　When these gray hairs of mine were brown—when
　　these dim eyes were bright.
A good wife came to meet me, and kiss me at the door,
　When weary with the day of toil I sought my home at
　　night.

Two children came to bless me, and my bright hearth
　brighter grew;
　To them I gave my day of strength, not thinkin' that
　　the night
Of old age might o'ertake me, and my true friends be
　few;
　And friends of old turn proud and cold and vanish
　　from my sight.

The wife who journeyed with me—the mother of my
　boys—
　Is sleepin' the long sleep of death; perhaps she now
　　looks down
Upon her aged partner—bereft of all his joys—
　A lodger in the station-house—a pauper on the town.

My boys ? Yes, they are livin'; and one is wealthy, too;
　IIe and his wife are movin' in a circle higher up;
To have the old man 'round was a thorn to her I knew;
　Her look of scorn, at night and morn, filled up my bit-
　　ter cup.

I've left them; I am goin' to a poorer son, out West;
　He does not know I'm comin', step by step, and all
　　alone;
IIe does not dream, at midnight, that his father takes
　his rest,
　Like peaceful, dreamin' Jacob, on a pillow made of
　　stone.

If I live to reach the threshold of their humble western
　cot,
　Though poor, I know their greetin' will not chill me
　　with its cold;
A dinner on a crust of bread, where love illumes the
　spot,
　Is better than a banquet where there's hatred for the
　　old.

I've seen, when on the ocean, a wreck upon the wave,
　Its masts, and rudder, all were gone, and not a soul
　　on board;
It drifted, drifted onward, as if seeking for a grave,
　While fiercely driving tempests thro' its shattered
　　bulwarks roared.

Thus on life's great storm-swept ocean, there are thous-
　ands poor and old,
　Who are drifting on the billows, or are driven thro'
　　the foam;

Who are looking—who are longing for the mansions
    built of gold—
  For the mercy, and the quiet of the sweet, eternal
    home.

Oh! To feel that you're a burden to the children you
    have reared,
  To know that they begrudge you every crust, and every
    bone,
Is like sitting in the shadows, when the grasses all are
    seared,
When the flowers all are faded and the summer birds
    have flown.

I thank you, kind policeman, for a bed upon the floor!
  I'll find a sweeter rest ere long, beyond the starry
    skies—
In the home that knows no winter—where they hunger
    never more—
  Where God shall wipe away the tears that dim my
    aged eyes.

NO MORTGAGE ON THE FARM.

MARY, let's kill the fatted calf and celebrate this
    day,
  For the last dreadful mortgage on the farm is
    wiped away;
    I have got the papers with me, they are right as
    right can be—
Let us laugh and sing together, for the dear old farm is
    free.

Don't all we Yankees celebrate the fourth day of July ?
Because 'twas then that freedom's sun lit up our nation's
    sky;
Why shouldn't we then celebrate, and this day ne'er
    forget ?
Where is there any freedom like being out of debt ?

I've riz up many mornin's an hour 'fore the sun,
And night has overtaken me before my task was done;
When weary with my labor 'twas this thought that
    nerved my arm,
Each day of toil will help to pay the mortgage on the
    farm.

And, Mary, you have done your part in rowin' to the
    shore,
By taking eggs and butter to the little village store;
You did not spend the money in dressin' up for show,
But sang from morn till evening in your faded calico.

And Bessy, our sweet daughter—God bless her loving
    heart,
The lad that gets her for a wife must be by nater smart—
She's gone without piano, her lonely hours to charm,
To have a hand in payin' off the mortgage on the farm.

I'll build a little cottage, soon, to make your heart re-
    joice;
I'll buy a good piano to go with Bessy's voice;
You shall not make your butter with that up and down
    concern,
For I'll go this very day and buy the finest patent churn.

Lay by your faded calico, and go with me to town,
And get yourself and Bessy a new and shinin' gown;
Low prices for our produce need not give us now alarm;
Spruce up a little, Mary! there's no mortgage on the
farm.

While our hearts are now so joyful, let us, Mary, not
forget
To thank the God of Heaven for being out of debt,
For He gave the rain and sunshine, and put strength
into my arm
And lengthened out our days to see no mortgage on the
farm.

THE RIGHT TO WORK TILL I DIE.

YOU needn't go showin' your patent right! don't
want such a thing on the farm;
I was born when they plowed with a wooden plow,
and the old thing worked like a charm;
Though my hands are bony and stiff with toil,
and dim is my failin' eye,
The only right I will have on the farm is the right to
work till I die.

"Buy that and I needn't work so hard"? that story a
dozen have told;
I've been wearin' out on this farm for years, I'll not rust
out now I'm old;
I was born in the days when men had to work, and I've
kinder got so now
That e'en in my dreams I am driving the teams, and
holdin' the well-worn plow.

A number of farmers 'round these parts are blossomin'
    out on the nose;
They call me a slow old-fogy now, and laugh at me I
    suppose;
I would rather move in my old-time way than to fly
    towards ruin's brink
By doin' my work up quick, like them, to hang 'round
    the town and drink.

"Save money by buyin' that thing of yours"? I've
    enough for Betsey and I,
and I've seen the evil of hoardin' gold, to be fought for
    after we die;
By doin' good to my fellow-men, as the Lord hath com-
    mandment given;
I've laid up treasures for many a year in the higher bank
    of heaven.

My farm numbered many acres once; I got along very
    well then,
For John took after his father for work, and so did my
    youngest, Ben;
They slipped their halters at twenty-one, and scampered
    off for a wife,
So I gave each a slice of the dear old farm and started
    them off in life.

If they work as the poor old man has worked—if they
    plan as he has planned—
They'll weather the storms, and enter the port, like a
    staunch old ship well manned;

I've learned in my life of three-score years—this thing—
among other things—
The riches we gain in the sweat of our brow are the riches
that grow no wings.

My farm is a very small one now; there is just enough
to do
To keep me busy from morn till night, the seedtime
and harvest through;
When Betsey and I lie under the sod—away from life's
hopes and fears—
Then John can work with the new machines where I've
cradled and mowed for years.

You're wastin' your time a talkin' with me—and time is
as good as gold—
I've been wearin' out on this farm for years—I'll not
rust out now I'm old;
So move along with your patent-right—some other fellow
try!
For the only right I'll have on the farm is the right to
work till I die.

❧

LIVE AND LET LIVE.

WELL! Farmer Smith has lost his wheat, his
sheds and mammoth barn:
His little boy, with one small match, burned up
the whole consarn;
I tell you wife, he'll feel it sore; a man on
money bent
Can't stand up under such a load when not insured a
cent.

I don't know as I pity him; I call it a great sin
To hoard the harvests of three years in spacious barn and
bin:
I can't feel pity for a man who double locks his door,
And stops his ears to all the cries that come up from the
poor.

I like to see economy; I like to see men save,
And lay up something for their kin when they are in
their grave:
But you and I know very well, from what we both have
seen,
That men can pinch and save until they're niggardly
and mean.

When wheat was sixteen shillings—a price that paid us
well—
Smith said "I'll wait for twenty, I vow, before I'll sell":
Then when it reached that figure, he said to me one
noon,
"I guess I'll hold it longer, 'twill be three dollars soon."

He held it, and he ran in debt for things to wear and eat;
When merchants dunned him he would say, "wait till I
sell my wheat."
Soon that old tune got fiddled out and men began to sue,
And he began to borrow to pay accounts long due.

When Smith goes off to buy a thing he runs around the
town,
And tries with all his might and main the price to banter
down;

When he has anything to sell 'tis priceless in his eyes,
And he must have the highest mark—the lowest when
    he buys.

"Live and let live" are golden words, this other motto,
    too,
"Do unto others as you wish that they would do to you:"
If Smith had done as they command he would not have,
    today,
The ashes of three harvests to load and draw away.

God bless the farmers of our land! They are not all like
    him,
Who walks around that smouldering pile, now, in the
    twilight dim;
Living on God's broad acres, their souls expand and
    grow;
Their ears ever open to tales of want and woe.

God bless the men, where'er they be, in country or in
    town,
Who do not think it life's great work to crowd their
    neighbors down!
This world would be the better, this life would pleasure
    give,
If every man who toils to live, would let his brother live.

HEAVEN AND HELL.

NOW, Betsey, it is my turn—now let the old man
    tell
Just how he looks at heaven, and what he thinks
    of hell;

For some men now are tellin', 'til nearly out of
  breath,
That everything is fixed up fine for sinners after death.

My years are three score years and ten—my hairs are
  white as snow;
I ought to know the ways of men—God's ways I ought
  to know:
I traveled on the downward road 'til conscience loud did
  cry,
"It is not all of life to live, nor all of death to die."

There is a hell, I know it, its fires are felt by some
Who leave their homes, and faithful wives, for harlots
  and for rum:
The fires of hell are kindled many years this side the
  grave;
They only burn the fiercer where no Christ can come to
  save.

There is a heaven, I feel it, an heaven begins below
When love to God and all mankind doth from the bosom
  flow:
The peace and joy that come to us along life's thorny
  way,
Are rays of light, to cheer the night, from heaven's eternal day.

No hell? Where, then is justice—Who'll settle with old
  Joe,
Who, with his whiskey, and his rum, is spreading want
  and woe ?

He took his poor old mother to the poorhouse, with a
frown,
And left her there to die, alone, a burden to the town.

Nor went he to the funeral—nor doth the hard man
know,
Or care where she is buried, who in childhood loved him
so;
A crony in his barroom, when he heard it, said in ire,
"When you go down to hell, old man, I'd like to poke
the fire."

No hell? There's Deacon Skinflint, with mortgages and
shares,
Devourin' widows' houses and for pretence making
prayers;
Shall he live on in luxury, wrung from the needy poor,
And then a crown, and harp of gold, at God's right hand
secure?

Let one of these new preachers take a starving widow's
place—
Let him feel the pangs of hunger, and the chill of Death's
embrace;
He then would leave his doctrine, and cry out, with
visage grim,
"Oh, Lord, remember Skinflint, and make a hell for him."

I tell you Betsey, it is hell to live with some men here,
And I may say some women, and no contradiction fear;
For I read in the old Bible I have learned to love so well,
"The tongue's a deadly poison and is set on fire of hell."

What would a guilty sinner do amid the angel choir?
To him the holiness of heaven would be the hottest fire;
Not all the golden harps above can make a happy place
For him who can not stand before the glory of God's face.

Not all the flowers of Paradise, not all the birds that
    sing,
Can moments of pure happiness to guilty sinners bring:
God is the bliss of Heaven; if He frowns upon the soul
'Tis fire, and endless torment, while eternal ages roll.

How many wicked men, through life, mount up on
    pleasure's wings,
While righteous men, who love their God, must bear
    affliction's stings;
How, then, can God be good to all, and just to all, as
    well,
If there's no heaven for godly men, for godless men no
    hell?

Ah! Betsey, let's be watchin', watchin' early, watchin' late!
Perchance a hungry Lazarus may come beggin' at our
    gate:
If so we'll bid him welcome, heal his wounds, and wipe
    his eyes,
For he who shows no mercy, gets no mercy when he dies.

"Oh happy day that fixed my choice"—that made my
    conscience cry,
"It is not all of life to live, nor all of death to die";
Let's trim our life lamps, Betsey,—keep 'em burnin'
    bright and clear,
For the midnight hour approaches—soon the bridegroom
    will be here.

THE OLD MAN GOES TO THE FAIR.

I'M very dusty and tired, wife! I've just come home
    from the fair;
So give me my pipe and tobacco, and I'll smoke in my
    easy chair;
It's tiresome work a playin' for feeble old men like me;
It's tiresome work a seein' where everyone wishes to see.

Our fairs are a runnin' down; they are not like the fairs
    of old,
Where you took the prizes for bread, and butter as yellow
    as gold;
There were hundreds of useful things that were well
    worth seein' then;
Now, dozens of racin' horses and hundreds of bettin'
    men.

What all this sportin' will lead to is more than I now
    can tell;
But, somehow, it seems to me like the downward road to
    h— well
I may be a little harsh, but I'm speaking' the simple
    truth,
For bettin', racin' and drinking are the foes of our
    noble youth.

We shall soon be a nation of gamblers, if matters keep on
    this way;
Why, what do you think? a youngster accused me of
    bettin' today;

When I laid my hand on the head—that hasn't seen ten
    years yet—
And called him a fine little fellow—he answered me back,
    "You bet!"

"Tut! tut!" little man, sad I, "that thing I never have
    done;
Come, stand by grandpa's knee! let me reason with you,
    my son.'
He straigthened up in his clothes, and said, with a look
    so queer,
"I didn't come here for preachin'; old man, walk off on
    your ear!"

We never heard talk like that when you and I were young;
My father and mother—bless 'em—put a bridle upon my
    tongue.
I'm old, and I'm gettin' blind, but a difference I can see
'Twixt the boys of eighteen-hundred, and eighteen-
    ninety-three.

How is it about the girls ? They, too, from the path
    have strayed;
I didn't see one a showin' the butter her hands had
    made;
They stood in their pony phætons, with woman's ease
    and grace,
And shouted as loud as any when a favorite won a race.

All eyes were watchin' the track; the race was every
    man's theme;
And I said, to myself, "Is this a fair, or is it only a
    dream ?"

I saw 'bout a dozen boys lookin' round at the sheep and
    swine,
And the frosts of seventy winters had silvered their
    heads like mine.

Why on airth don't they change the name, when the
    wrong name it has got?
No longer call it a fair, but an agricultural trot;
Then men won't be takin' things for sensible folks to see,
With nobody there to see 'em but crippled old men like
    me.

There, take my pipe and tobacco! I'll sleep in my easy
    chair;
It's tiresome work a-talkin' about a degenerate fair;
You needn't disturb me, wife, till the bells of evening
    chime,
For I may go back in my dreams to the fairs of the olden
    time.

THE PREACHER'S VACATION.

OUR preacher gone huntin' and fishin'? Gone off
    his vacation to take?
Well, Nancy, that sounds rather funny to a man
    of the old fashioned make:
    The news sets my old brain a-thinkin' of the olden-
      time preachers again,
Who didn't go fishin' for fishes, for the Lord made them
    "fishers of men."

Worn out is he, preachin' on Sunday, and visitin'
'round through the week ?
For a rest from his arduous labor in wood and by streams
must he seek ?
If a stray sheep should bleat for the shepherd—if a sinner
should turn from his sin—
Who will open the door of the Kingdom to welcome the
prodigal in ?

If an angel with dazzlin' pinions should stop in his
heavenward flight
And take from the cradle a baby to the sweet home that
knoweth no night,
Who will comfort the heart of the mother with the words
that a preacher can say ?
Who will read from the Bible a chapter and kneel by the
coffin to pray ?

Must the prodigal go to the forest to hunt up the winner
of souls ?
Alone must the mother sit weeping while sorrows wave
over her rolls ?
What account will the shepherd be givin', when cometh
the reckonin' day,
For the precious time wasted in huntin' and down by the
rivers at play ?

Why, Nancy, the old-fashioned elders could preach every
day in the week;
They rode their long circuits o'er mountains in weather
tempestuous and bleak.

No rest knew the pioneer preachers from labors of duty
    and love,
'Till the Good Shepherd called them up higher, to man-
    sions eternal above.

They studied their sermons from nature; a voice had the
    birds and the brooks;
The Bible without note or comment to them was the Book
    of all books.
When they stood in the rude school-house pulpit the
    Lord touched their lips with the fire
And the simple songs sung by the people were caught by
    the heavenly choir.

Old Paul never had a vacation — never idled his moments
    away—
Though the great care of all of the churches lay on his
    brave heart every day.
The prison walls echoed his singing; he preached 'till he
    sat himself down
And cried "I have fought a good fight! Henceforth
    there is laid up my crown!"

Some men are deservin' a respite from labors of body and
    mind;
In every good work they are foremost—the world never
    finds them behind:
They preach burnin' words from the pulpit; they write
    golden words for the press;
And their names are a joy in the households of the land
    they are livin' to bless.

Well, Nancy, the world is a changin'! Old ways and old
    people die out;
It will not help matters I'm thinkin' for old men to set
    down and pout:
Some changes have made the world better; some changes
    have brought the world loss;
But the way that now leadeth to heaven is still the old
    way of the Cross.

POEMS.

YE gray old woods of Genesee,
　　Leafless and carpeted with snow,
　　No more shall youthful friends with me
　　　Through all thy winding pathways go;
　　How desolate and lonely now
Are places once a sweet retreat,
Where, neath the shady maple bough,
We sat to rest our weary feet.

We carved our names upon the trees
　　That offered us the cooling shade,
And sent our shouts upon the breeze,
　　Laughing, to hear the echoes made.
Then ran we down the narrow trails,
　　Pushing the tangled bushes back,
And, in the opening filled our pails
　　With tempting berries, red and black.

How many times, with shouldered gun,
　　We in thy shade have listening stood,
Watching, to see the squirrel run
　　That barked so loudly in the wood.
And when the night came creeping on,
　　Returning from our hunting, lame,
Charley, laughing, says to John
　　"Your powder's gone, but where's your game?"

Ye gray old woods of Genesee,
   No season of the rolling year
Could rob our hearts of love for thee,
   Or keep our feet from coming here.
Old winter, with his storm and sleet,
   Forbade us lingering in the wood,
We strapped our skates upon our feet
   And bade him harm us if he could.

No more those youthful friends with me
   Shall in thy winding pathways tread;
Our names have faded from the tree,
   And two that carved them there, are dead.
No more shall ring our merry shout,
   From forest shade to green hillside,
For death has put the life lamp out,
   And rowed those friends across the tide.

When stormy clouds of war arose,
   And Union men from hill and dell
Marched forth to meet their country's foes,
   They bravely fought and bravely fell;
One, sleepeth in the distant West;
   Another by the restless sea;
No more thy shade shall give them rest,
   Ye gray old woods of Genesee.

THE OLD MAN'S CREED.

WIFE, listen! Don't you hear them—the holy
    Sabbath bells?
Up from the distant city how the joyous music
    swells:
They are calling folks together 'neath the
    temple's lofty dome,
But you and I must worship in the quiet of our home.

It makes but little difference about the time or place:
In city full, and wilderness, God hath a throne of grace;
It matters very little where the head is bowed in prayer,
If the heart is only contrite, God will meet man anywhere.

I've sat here many Sabbaths, since my three-score years
    and ten,
A-studyin' God's holy word and thinkin' about men;
I've often listened to those bells, while each one seemed
    to say,
Lo, here is Christ! Lo, here is Christ, and this the
    ancient way.

There are Jews in Christian churches who will have no
    deal today
With another Christian brother, if he's from Samaria:
I'm sick of the profession that doth say with knitted brow
To another toiler, "Stand aside, I'm holier than thou!"

I've lived too many years, dear wife, by words to be
    enticed;
I love all Christians who by deeds exalt a risen Christ;
I'm dead opposed to any church, whate'er the name may
    be,
That lets her zeal for doctrines override her Charity.

God hasn't time to listen to hear about a creed
While there are sinners to be saved, and weary hearts
    that bleed;
The Lord of glory didn't die to build up a belief;
He came to save the fallen—to give burdened souls relief.

Good deeds, instead of doctrines, is the world's great
    need today;
He who has the Master's spirit need not worry 'bout the
    way:
I think when I see Christians stand and argue, face to face,
They've a deal of human nater and a very little grace.

"Bear ye one another's burdens" says the great apostle
    Paul;
And what he said to one church he surely meant for all;
We might have another Pentecost, a shower from the
    Lord,
If Christians, all, of every name, would work with one
    accord.

We may take a wayside thistle and give names to all its
    twigs,
'Twill be a pesky thistle, still, and never bear us figs:
To visit the afflicted —to keep from sin unstained—
Is how the starry crown is won; the pearly gates are
    gained.

From this church, and from that church, the good at
    last will come,
An' 'twill be a joyful meetin' when they all arrive at
    home;
From this church, and from that church, will come up
    the men of creeds,
And Christ will say "I know ye not, ye did no Christian
    deeds."

The blessed day is comin' when all Christians will be one;
We may not live to see it for our race is nearly run;
The blessed day is comin', I can see the dawning light
That shall drive away the darkness of sectarianism's
    night.

I've tried to love all Christians, these fifty years and
    more;
When I die I know the Master will say to me, at the door,
"Inasmuch as ye have done it unto one of these, the least,
Ye have done unto me; enter now into my feast."

PRAYED HIM OUT.

THE shutters are up at the windows; the bolt is
    turned now in the door
Of the groggery on the corner, that few have seen
    closed before;
    For the women came from their dwellings and
        gathered the shop about
And Tom slid out the back door, for the women soon
    prayed him out.

We've arrested that fellow, and fined him, more times
than I've fingers and toes,
But we never could stop, for a moment, his fountain of
human woes:
With the money he made on his whisky he well could
afford to pay;
But he didn't know how to meet the foe that came to
his bar to pray.

We've tried on him moral suasion; we've pictured the
ruin wrought
In the peaceful homes of our village; but our labor has
been for naught;
"Somebody will sell if I don't," was his time-worn rock
of defence
Against our strongest arguments—our volleys of common
sense.

Tom Murphy could stand the pressure when one woman
came alone,
To pray and weep in his barroom—to plead with his
heart of stone,
But when they came down in battalions and knelt on his
barroom floor,
The shutters went up at the windows—the key turned
the bolt in the door.

Tom Murphy has bribed our judges—has bought all our
juries, too;
Our single prayers and entreaties he stubbornly waded
through;
But the giant of Castle Ruin has fled from his work away,
For he couldn't buy off the women who knelt on his floor
to pray.

Don't squibble about who did it; enough that the work
   is done;
And mothers shall seek at Murphy's no more for a
   ruined son;
The lawyers, and moral suasion, may be able some folks
   to route,
But give us the praying women who prayed Tom Murphy
   out.

THE BURNING OF BOSTON.

FIRE! fire! ashes! ashes!
   O'er the land the sad news flashes;
   Ashes! ashes! ruin! ruin!
   Flames are man's grand work undoing;
   Flames, like tongues from pit infernal,
Wield the power of the eternal;
   Flames, fierce flames that feel no pity,
Mounting upward, higher rise,
   'Til they paint a burning city
On the canvas of the skies;
   Flames, fierce flames that feel no pity,
Ride o'er dwellings bad and good,
   'Till they leave a fallen city
Where a famous city stood.
     Fire! fire!
     Touch the wire!
Send the news from state to state;
Comes the fire fiend in his ire;
Boston meets Chicago's fate!

Higher! higher!
Higher than the burning tower
Rises a great nation's pity
For a well beloved city
All on fire;
Writhing in the demon's power,
Waves of words all sympathetic—
Waves of actions energetic—
Flood toward the smoking city
Now in this her darkest hour;
Waves from cot and costly dwelling
Flooding onward, loud are telling,
"Still abide the blessed three—
Faith, and hope, and charity;
Still the greatest, charity."
Fire! fire!
Touch the wire!
O'er the land the tidings send;
Comes the fire-fiend in his ire;
Boston finds Chicago's friend.

Lift the head bowed down with sorrow!
Dead? The city is not dead!
Boston shall arise tomorrow
Lovely from her ashen bed;
Flames may revel,
Flames may level
Granite wall and lofty spire,
But the spirit of the people
Cannot be consumed by fire;
Flames may revel,
Flames may level

Lowly cot and stately hall;
Time shall ressurrect them all;
All the spires that caught the morning,
 And the gold from sunset skies;
All that once was her adorning
 From these ashes shall arise;
Like the staunch ship on the ocean,
 Waves may foam, and clouds may frown,
Storms may check her onward motion,
 But the good ship goes not down;
  Flames have reveled,
  Flames have leveled
Granite wall and lofty spire,
 But the old Bostonian spirit
Has not been consumed by fire;
 Touch the wire!
Send the news from shore to shore!
 Though the fire-fiend did o'ertake her,
 Boston lives, and time shall make her
All she was in days of yore!

A TALE OF THE BOY WITH WINGS.

THERE'S news again in the town, wife; 't is a tale
  of the boy with wings;
Love laughs again at the locksmith, and all his in-
  tricate springs;
 For a maiden—an only daughter—shut in by
  his bolts and bars,—
Has gone away with her lover, in the light of the twinklin' stars.

Shut in by a father's hand, from the gaze of a "portion-
less boy,"
Whose tender eyes had thrilled the maiden's heart with
joy;
Shut in with an angry frown, and the youth shut out
with a curse;
The father had chosen a lover, with lands and a weighty
purse.

But the heart is a stubborn thing; its doors and ways are
its own;
The strongest fail, by force, its idols to dethrone;
The father found his daughter's thus; though his will
and bolts were stout,
He could not force a new love in, nor fasten the old love
out.

In the light of the twinklin' stars, the youth with the
tender eyes
Came back to the fair one's home and captured his
precious prize;
Away, through the sleepin' town, over hills and frozen
streams,
They fled from her prison home to the goal of their
youthful dreams.

There the priest, with holy words, pronounced them man
and wife;
Then the day dawned in the east, with the dawn of a
brighter life,
And the angels sang 'mid the stars the same triumph
song
They have sung for many ages, at a victory over wrong.

When will parents cease to barter their flesh and blood
    for gold;
When will matches cease to be made where hearts are
    dead and cold ?
Until the dawn of a brighter day shall gladden this world
    of ours,
Love will laugh at the toiling locksmith from his home
    'mid the deathless flowers.

Long live the happy wife who hath chosen the better part,
In turning her back on mammon, for the love of an
    honest heart!
Long live the brave young man, who, despite the bolts
    and bars,
Won his bride, and carried her off in the light of the
    twinklin' stars!

BEAUTIFUL MAY—A SONG.

I MET her in the meadow green,
When sunlight on the hills was seen;
She looked as lovely as a queen;
Ah! I remember well the day,
The flowers blossomed on our way,
But she was fairer, far, than they.

Chorus.

Beautiful May, life glideth away
We'll meet o'er the river,
My beautiful May.

We told our love with laughing eyes,
Beneath the cloudless summer skies,
When singing larks did upward rise;
I looked within her eyes of blue
And saw that they were cloudless, too;
Her love for me was warm and true.

Now, ever in my memory,
Her face and sunny smile I see,
For she was all the world to me;
And oft times when the world is dark,
Her angel form doth guide my bark—
I hear the old time singing lark.

The time will come when we shall meet,
Beyond this life so incomplete—
Where hearts with sorrow never beat;
Oh! on that bright and glorious day,
I there shall greet my lovely May,
Where earth-born sorrows fade away.

CHARITY.

OH! Charity, sister of heavenly birth,
Come spread thy bright wings o'er a tempest-
swept earth;
Make us slow to believe all the evil we hear;
Make us quick to forgive at the penitent tear.

Great hearts are now bleeding, and sweet homes are dark;
For the bright flame of love has gone down to a spark.
If thou hadst but dwelt there, oh! Charity, bright,
Those hearts and those homes would have gathered no
    night.

Oh! Charity, sister of heavenly birth,
Come gather the thorns from the pathways of earth;
For jealousy, envy, and hatred, now sweep
O'er the households of earth like a storm o'er the deep.

Our natures are fallen; our hearts take delight
In seeing a brother enshrouded in night;
Ere we are aware we add dregs to his bowl,
And deepen the shadows that darken his soul.

The clouds of suspicion do often enfold
Great men whose true hearts are as pure as the gold;
Thou, Charity, stayest the voice of the crowd
Till proven the guilt, or is lifted the cloud.

Oh, Charity, sister of heavenly birth,
Come spread thy bright wings o'er the hearth-stones of
    earth.
Make our feet swift to run to the rescue of him
Who falls in the shadows where daylight is dim.

Make us slow to believe all the evil we hear;
Make us quick to forgive at the penitent tear.
Teach us, all, who 'mid pitfalls and shadows do live,
That 'tis human to err, but divine to forgive.

HOMEWARD O'ER ONTARIO'S WAVE.

FAST the land is disappearing
　　As we plow Ontario's wave;
　　Home and friends I'm swiftly nearing—
　　Cherished friends, both fair and brave;
Ere the night shall cast her shadows,
　The green fields and blue waves o'er,
We'll espy the hills and meadows
　Of Columbia's lovely shore.

Farewell bright Canadian waters!
　Farewell wooded hill and dell!
We'll remember the fair daughters
　Seen where billows gently swell,
Other maidens will be singing
　Songs of sadness, songs of glee,
When the evening chimes are ringing
　By the flowing Genesee.

Fast the paddle-wheels are beating
　The blue waters into foam.
Oh! how sweet will be the meeting
　With the little ones at home;
When their tiny arms caress me,
　And I catch their loving kiss,
What can I ask, more, to bless me
　In a weary world like this?

Hark! The harbor bells are ringing
  We can hear them where we stand
Every paddle-stroke is bringing
  The brave steamer nearer land;
Night is letting down her shadows
  The green fields and blue waves o'er;
Hail, all hail, ye hills and meadows
  Of Columbia's lovely shore.

SPIRIT RAPPINGS IN LONDON.

A COUSIN I have; a great joker is he;
  The fun-light is seen in the glance of his eye;
He was born in a beautiful land o'er the sea,
  Where the sweet-scented primroses blossom
      and die;
His name it is Nicholas, but, to be quick,
We shorten it up by calling him Nick.

He labored in London for many a year,
  Learning his trade at the best of schools;
Through some of the days of his youth, I fear,
  He played more with tricks than he did with tools;
But some men are born, and live and die,
With a roguish look and a laughing eye.

A lone widow lived near the dwelling of Nick;
  She was timid—as widows are wont to be—
She dreaded a ghost, and her pulse beat quick,
  If anything strange she did hear or see—
Her midnight dreams, and her noon day nappings
Were often disturbed by mysterious rappings.

Nick knew this well, so what did he do
　　But capture a cat, running wild in the street?
And taking his carpenters' pot of glue,
　　Stuck nut-shells on to the old cat's feet;
Then, telling the feline to grin and bear it,
Let her loose at night in the widow's garret.

Pit-te-pat, pit-te-pat, "O! dear, what was that?"
　　The widow cried out as she covered her head;
" 'Tis a spirit, I know, from the regions of woe,
　　Perhaps 'tis my husband returned from the dead;
Had I scolded him less, had I used him well here,
My life would not now be tormented with fear."

Pit-te-pat, pit-te-pat, went the shell-footed cat,
　　Through garret and chamber, through kitchen and hall,
Seeking, not for a mouse, but escape from the house,
　　Escape from the strange house that held her in thrall,
The cat and the widow, both nervous with fright,
Neither one slept a wink through the long, weary night.

A morning serene at last dawned on the scene,
　　But the rappings fled not with the darkness of night;
So the widow peeped out, when the ghost moved about,
　　And quickly she saw to her soul's great delight
That the spirit that made her faint heart faster beat
Was only an old cat with shells on her feet.

There are thousands, today, led in error away,
　　By things that, in darkness, no mortal can trace;
But when, through the night, cometh truth's shining light,
　　It all is as plain as the nose on your face;
Errors, played in the dark, when the truth they must meet,
Are as harmless as poor cats with shells on their feet.

THE TEARLESS LAND.

OUR floral forget-me-nots blossom and die,
When the winds of the autumn sweep chillingly by;
But the heart's bright forget-me-nots never shall
fade
When under the white drifts our loved ones are
laid;
And the days, as they fly o'er the dial of time,
Are bringing us nearer to that brighter clime
Where we shall again our lost loved ones embrace
And the glories of home shall earth's sorrows efface.

We weave from fair blossoms a cross and a crown,
And on the cold coffin we lay them both down;
'Tis all we can do; we'll adorn the fair clay
Ere under the white drifts we lay it away.
But the days, as they fly o'er the dial of time,
Are bringing us nearer to that brighter clime
Where the crowns are not leaves that must wither and
mold,
But they sparkle with jewels and glisten with gold.

We sing our sweet hymns round the slumbering clay
Ere under the white drifts we lay it away;
And we lift our dim eyes to the kingdom above,
Unto Him who chastiseth us only in love.
O! the days, as they fly o'er the dial of time,
Are bringing us nearer to that brighter clime
Where the songs of the blest with the sainted we'll sing
At the feet of our Prophet, our Priest, and our King.

We bury the dead we so love from our sight,
While a star beameth forth from the depths of our night;
It comforts the heart, and dispelleth the gloom,
As we follow the dead to the rest of the tomb.
O! the days, as they fly o'er the dial of time,
Are bringing us nearer to that brighter clime
Where "the King in his beauty," the Bethlehem Star,
Shall cheer us forever in kingdoms afar.

OUT ON NIAGARA'S WATERS.

THE moonlit nights are with us now;
The cool breeze fans the heated brow;
From business free, our glad hearts sing
Like larks that from the meadows spring;
Our voices echo as we glide
Along Niagara's moonlit tide.

Hark to the music! how it fills
The nooks of the Canadian hills;
The voices of our loved ones, dear,
Sound in the night air sweet and clear;
With happy hearts we onward glide,
Along Niagara's moonlit tide.

Ye waters of this rushing stream,
Dance on, and in the moonlight gleam;
The rapids soon shall dash thee o'er
The precipice with deaf'ning roar,
Now, in the moonlight, laugh away,
'Till rocks shall dash thee into spray.

Oh! bright Niagara's moonlit tide,
Like thee, through Life, we onward glide;
In youth our hearts, like ripples, laugh,
As we our youth-time pleasures quaff;
Soon cares, like rocks, hedge up our way,
And dash our pleasures into spray;
In age we call our life a breath,
And leap the precipice of death.

THE LESSON OF THE SPARROWS.

"HARD times, hard times!" I hear it
    'Bout everywhere I go;
In mansions of the wealthy,
    And hovels of the low;
In stores among the merchants,
Where factory wheels are still;
"Hard times, hard times!" is echoed
    From every barren hill.

Well, what's the use of fretting,
    Or giving way to fears?
We cannot mourn the clouds away,
    Nor bridge a stream with tears;
When darkness gathers 'round us,
    And brings us loss or pain,
Keep Hope's lamp brightly burning
    Until day dawns again.

When swift the stream is running,
　And near the breaker roars,
Then set your feet down firmly
　And pull hard on the oars:
Luck starves upon the wayside,
　Pluck bravely hopes and sings,
And trudges o'er the rugged road,
　To feast at last, with kings.

The skies will soon grow brighter,
　And hard times pass away;
The night is always darkest
　Near the dawning of the day;
Hold on a little longer,
　There is light and joy ahead,
For be it known, from hut to throne,
　God isn't lost or dead.

One day while homeward walking,
　I saw a cracker fall,
When down came many sparrows
　From nests along the wall;
They quickly filled their little crops,
　And in their way they said;
"We thank thee, kind Creator,
　For this our daily bread."

If God cares for the sparrows,
　The weary winter through,
Oh, thou who art of greater worth,
　Shall he not care for you?
Hold on a little longer;
　There's light and joy ahead!
For, soon, the factory's spinning wheels
　Will give you daily bread.

THE OLD BELL FOUNDER.

THE old bell founder! years ago,
  He lived within our town:
He was a man of no great means,
  A man of no renown;
Oft have I lingered near his shop,
To hear the sweet tones swell,
As he would test, with measured stroke,
A newly-moulded bell.

Long years ago, my old friend died;
  A man of no renown—
His lands were sold to other men,
  His little shop—pulled down;
But, ere he passed away from earth,
  Or felt Death's dreaded power,
One of his bells was hung within
  A Sanctuary's tower.

Now, every Sabbath day, its tones
  Ring out so sweet, and clear,
Calling the many worshippers
  In God's house to appear.
Oft do I think of that old man;
  Of work he done so well;
Though dead, I feel he liveth, still,
  In that sweet-sounding bell.

There is a life we all may live;
    A work we all may do;
That will some joy and comfort give,
    When life's short day is through;
The good deeds done, the kind words said,
    The earthly life lived well;
May speak to others, when we're dead,
    Like that sweet-sounding bell.

ON THE NORSEMAN.

YEARS fly by; again I'm standing
    On the Norseman, staunch and true;
    With a genial man commanding,
    Soon we'll cleave the waters blue:
Farewell now to care and sorrow
That has swept my heart strings o'er;
When shall dawn the bright tomorrow,
    We shall touch Ontario's shore.

Hark! the steamer's whistle blowing!
    Quiet waters gently swell;
Now the paddle wheels are going,
    Charlotte harbor, fare-thee-well!
Fare-the-well, green shores and meadows
    Of the land I love the best,
Soon within Canadian shadows,
    By the streams I'll sweetly rest.

Bright the harbor lights are burning
    All along the fading shore,
As my thoughts are backward turning,
    To the loved I'll see no more;

Years ago I came to meet them,
   Where those harbor lights now burn;
On the Norseman I did greet them,
   Joyful o'er their safe return.

Life and children now are sleeping
   Peacefully within the grave;
All alone my watch I'm keeping,
   As I cross Ontario's wave.
But the years are swiftly flying,
   Soon my feet shall touch the shore
Where my heart shall cease its sighing
   For the dear ones gone before.

HYMN TO NIAGARA.

OH! Royal, grand Niagara,
   God's greatest wonder-king
I stand beneath thy falling spray
   My hymn of praise to sing;
I walk around thy royal head,
   And view thy misty crown,
Or and and gaze with awe and dread,
   To where thy waves go down.

Sumptuous it may seem in me,
   A bard of humble birth,
To sing a hymn of praise to thee,
   Thou wonder of the earth;

But God hath made thee for us all,
   And high of birth, and low,
May see thy billows plunge and fall
   To the far depths below.

Oh! when did first thy song begin,
   The listener to entrance?
What race stood in the dim, old wood
   Thy wondering audience?
Methinks when the last trump shall sound,
   And time shall be no more,
The angels in the final hymn,
   Shall hear thy billows roar.

Oh! Royal, grand Niagara,
   The God who rules thy tide
Shall guide the good man on his way,
   And journey by his side;
And when thy waves shall cease to plunge
   And leap this precipice,
His soul, in brighter worlds, afar,
   Shall but begin its bliss.

Roll on thou grand Niagara!
   Leap on to depths below!
Sing to the great Creator's praise
   To these who come and go,
Sing, 'til the great arch-angel's voice
   The sleeping dead shall raise,
And the destruction of the earth
   Shall end thy hymn of praise.

THE CONFLICT OF LIFE.

GREAT souls have gone down where the tempest
was wailing—
　　Gone down with the faults and the virtues they
　　bore;
　Too near hidden rocks they were constantly sail-
　ing—
Too near where the breakers terrifically roar.

Great souls have shot up to the heavens in glory,
　Like rockets that burst and are lost to the sight:
Their life's end, when told, makes a pitiful story;
　They shone well but fell in the darkness of night.

Great souls have been vanquished in life's raging battle,
　By foes that were secretly lurking within;
They were strong in the conflict—where leaden shots
　rattle,
But weak in the fight with temptation and sin.

Great souls—like the stars that from heaven are shooting,
　Have fallen from places of honor and trust;
Like fine trees of promise that died ere their fruiting,—
　Like half-opened buds broken down in the dust

When telling their story, Oh! do not remember
　The faults of the good soul that finally fails!
The May of his life may outweigh the December
　If sweet, loving Charity holdeth the scales.

Thy feet on a rock, reach thy hand to a brother
  Who vainly endeavors to battle the wave,
For thou are but mortal, and some day or other
  Thy voice, thro' the storm, may be calling to save.

⚘

EXTERNAL AND INTERNAL.

WE cannot, always, merit tell
    By what we see external;
  For, often, 'neath the roughest shell,
    We find the sweetest kernel.

By ocean storm, with thunder shock,
  O'er hidden pearls, we're ferried;
Beneath the sand, and rugged rock,
  The precious gold lies buried.

The book that flashes golden sparks,
  And hides the thoughts worth finding,
Will soon be soiled by finger marks,
  And have a ragged binding.

The men who swing their dandy canes,
  Nice attitudes asssuming,
Are seldom overstocked with brains,
  And, therefore, need perfuming.

The world's eye, doth the outward scan,
  And not the hidden kernel;
The man, that God has a stamped a man,
  Is always good internal.

COME TO ME.

OH come to me, come to me beautiful flowers,
Spring forth from the sod in the dim woodland
  bowers!
I'm weary of seeing the ice and the snow,
  I'm weary of hearing the winter winds blow,
The joy of my heart shall beam forth from my eyes,
When daises and pansies look up to the skies.

Oh come to me, come to me days that are glad!
When the elm and the maple in green shall be clad
When the pale, wasted cheek of the suffering one
Can catch the soft breeze in the warmth of the sun;
The joy of my heart shall beam forth from my eyes
When the lark from his nest in the meadow shall rise.

The months of real summer are fleeting and few,
As precious as friends who are tender and true;
Oh come to me then, at my welcoming words,
Ye days that are sunny, ye blossoms and birds!
The joy of my heart shall beam forth from my eyes,
When daisies and pansies look up to the skies.

Oh come to me, come to me, Lord of my love!
I've no one below, I have no one above,
That can for a moment, my heart satisfy
Like the one who, to save me, was willing to die;
The joy of my heart shineth forth from my face
For the arm of the Lord doth the weary embrace.

THE BEAUTIFUL HOUSE THAT BRIBERY BUILT.

IT stands on a broad street shaded by trees
That bend to the blast, and bow to the breeze;
'Tis an elegant house, with French plate glass,
Admired by lovers of art who pass;
There the robins sing through the summer days,
And the bells, on the Sabbath, join their praise;
To the dewy eve from the early dawn
The green grass grows on the level lawn;
No wonder the poor in amazement stand
And sigh for a house so large and grand;
But an infamous deed has tarnished its gilt—
'Tis a beautiful house by bribery built.

But what careth he who enters its door ?
He pocketed forty thousand or more
For a single vote; he can well afford
To walk like a duke and live like a lord
The money he gained is more to him
Than an honored name that groweth not dim;
He taketh his ease, amid glitter and gilt,
In the beautiful house that bribery built.

Toll, toll ye bells in the towers nigh!
Ye toll when the bodies of men do die;
Then why not toll on the air o'erhead,
When a man's good name is forever dead ?
When honor and honesty, both, are lost,
Has man anything of which to boast ?

Is there no higher good to win
Than dollars that bear the stamp of sin ?
Does it matter not how our wealth we gain ?
Is it better to win and wear a stain
Than walk in the humble walks of life,
An honest man in the world's great strife ?
Must we bow the knee to the man of guilt
In the beautiful house that bribery built ?

A poor man steals but a loaf of bread
For a starving child, his name is dead;
And he looketh out on the evening stars
And sighs for home from the prison bars;
Shall men high up in the people's trust
Sell out their votes for the briber's dust,
And then return to their homes again
To walk in the ranks of honored men ?
No, no! For the gold, men wrongly gain.
Will leave on the soul a damning stain;
Nor beautiful house, nor gold, nor time
Can wipe from the page the blot of crime;
Forever, forever a cloud of guilt
O'ershadows the house that bribery built;
And men shall call it, with blush of shame,
"The monument of a dead good name."

In vain he walketh with lifted head—
A corpse in its tomb is not more dead;
If he thinks he lives, let him from the dust
Arise, and ask for a place of trust.
The people will point to the damning blot
And shout, "Depart, for we know you not!
Back, back again to your tomb of guilt
In the beautiful house that bribery built!"

O! when shall we see the dawning day
When office-seekers shall not hold sway ?
When men shall adopt the better plan
Of the office seeking the upright man ?
When that day dawns—when thus we do—
Never again shall glitter and gilt
Tower on high 'neath skies of blue,
A beautiful house by bribery built.

LIFE'S LESSONS.

No. 1.

THEY shall win in lengthy races,
Who keep firmly on the road;
Pulling steady in the traces
Is what draws the heavy load;
Silent, unperceived, the motion,
See how God's creation works;
Where would be the land or ocean
If the world went round by jerks.

Some men, in their life behavior,
Show at times a spirit meek;
Some work Sunday for the Saviour
Then are idle all the week.
These are not the men of battle,
Who pull giant evil down;
These are they who shun the rattle,
And, in shunning, lose the crown.

Constant dropping, steady hewing,
  Wears the solid rock away;
So shall we, one end pursuing,
  Reap reward that shall repay.
Ah! it is the steady workers,
  That with honey fill the hive;
Let us, then, no more be jerkers,
  But by steady pulling thrive.

Little spring-brooks in the meadow
  Flow, when mountain streams are dry;
Cattle sleeping in the shadow,
  But for these would faint and die;
Let your deeds of love flow steady,
  Though they may to you look small;
Thus thy soul shall be made ready,
  When the messenger shall call.

LIFE'S LESSONS.

No. 2.

STRONG are the habits that we form
    When we are young in years;
  They go with us through sun and storm;
    They bring us joy or tears.
    And as the days go flying past,
  These habits stronger grow,
Until they bring the soul at last
  To blessedness or woe.

The vessel that doth badly leak,
  E'er land is lost to view,
When ocean storms in thunders speak,
  Goes down with all the crew.

If evil habits gain control,
    When youthful skies are clear,
How shall we fare when billows roll,
    And the dark night draws near ?

Beginning well is half the race;
    And he shall surely win,
Who, with strong hands and cheerful face,
    Doth rightly life begin.
Yes, he who learns to rightly do,
    In youth's formation time,
Shall be to God and mankind true,
    And make his life sublime.

One little word will often save,
    When tempted wrong to go;
At such a time be strong, be brave,
    And firmly answer, No!
It takes a hero in the strife,
    That little word to say;
Well, heroes win the better life,
    That crowns the better way

LIFE'S LESSONS.

No. 3.

GOD made you for a certain place:
    Your neighbor for another;
Then meet him with a smiling face,
    And treat him like a brother.

What though his place be higher up,
    And yours a lower station;
His may not be the sweeter cup,
    Nor yours the meaner ration.

God gives responsibility
  With talents shining brightly:
And wakeful hours, you may not see,
  Are with some toilers, nightly.

How watchful, when the billow heaves
  Must be the lighthouse keeper;
And he must bring home golden sheaves
  Whom God hath made a reaper.

On heads that wear the diadem
  Black hairs to gray are turning,
Your place would be so sweet to them,
  Their hearts for rest are yearning.

Work in the harness and the place
  That God to you hath given;
And you shall see Him, face to face,
  Mid brighter scenes in Heaven.

❧

TO MOTHER IN HEAVEN.

MOTHER in Heaven, thy loving ways
  Are thought of oft in my pilgrim days;
The words of warning and council given,
  By lips of thine to me,
Like golden cords, through the gates of heaven,
  Are leading me home to thee.

Mother, the daisies you planted there,
In the round bed, with the lilies fair,

I moved them to a brighter place,
  To give them the sun and dew;
For I knew that God, with his dying grace,
  Had done the same by you.

Mother, thy name is repeated oft,
By loving lips in accents soft;
They tell how they miss your gentle tread,
  And the hands so quick to do,
When called to the sick, the dying, the dead,
  The day, and the long night through.

I know that many mothers, good,
Have nobly by their life-task stood,
Until, by storms, to the harbor driven,
  They have gone with the saints to be,
And others are setting their sails for Heaven,
  But none do out-shine thee.

A GOOD NAME.

A good name is rather to be chosen than great
riches.—Bible.

LIKE the eternal hills that tower
    In grandeur to the very sky,
    Yet tremble not, before the power
    Of tempests sweeping madly by,
      So shall a good name ever stand;
    No slanders vile can it destroy;
  Unmoved, it lives, like mountain-land,
    A beauty, and a lasting joy

It is a gem, that sparkles bright
    When gold cannot enjoyment bring;
It is a star, that cheers the night,
    When lost, to man, seems everything.
Our garments worn, we cast aside;
    Changing are all things that we see;
A good name, brightens, as the tide
    Sweeps on toward eternity.

Be careful of thy soul-bright star;
    Young man, to thy good name be just;
Thou, only cans't its beauty mar,
    And bring it, ruined, to the dust;
'Twill buy thee, in a trying hour,
    What glittering gold can never buy;
'Twill save thee, by its blessed power,
    When rolling waves of death are nigh.

LITTLE WINGS.

The last words of little Lillian J. Crosby, aged four years and nine months, are worthy of being long remembered. She was the sweet, gentle playmate of my precious Walter, now at rest in the beautiful home. The day before little Lillian died, she said to her weeping mother: "If I die I'll go to heaven where Walter is; Walter's got little wings, and I'll have little wings, and sometimes I'll fly down and see you, mamma."

SOMETIMES I'll fly down to you, mamma,
    From my home in the Morning Land;
And when you are weary, and faint, and sad,
    Unseen by your side I'll stand;

On your lips I will print a spirit kiss,
And nestle down close to your heart,
Till you sigh to be gone from a world like this,
To the home where they never part.

"Sometimes I'll fly down to you, mamma,
With one of the angel, ties,
And I'll fasten it firm to the loving hearts
That are heavy with mournful sighs;
Then back to the Morning Land I'll go
And fast to the tie I'll hold,
'Til I lead you away from this vale of woe
To my home in the city of gold.

"Sometimes I'll fly down to you, mamma,
For heaven is not so far;
The angels can come in a little time
From the farthest twinkling star."
Oh! Lillian Lillian, precious child!
We are tossing on Life's dark sea;
May we live aright, though the night be wild
Then fly away up to thee.

❧

THE RIVER FERRY.

A FERRY-BOAT crosses the river of death
To the far-off, viewless shore;
And men go aboard, at their latest breath,
And are seen on earth no more;
And the friends of the passengers weep and moan
As the boat floats off to the dim unknown.

A rich man came down to the river of death
  With his heavy bags of gold;
The ferry-boat waited, with smoking breath,
  Afloat on the waters cold;
The shadows grew deeper, the dark waves roared,
As he begged them to carry his gold on board.

"We ferry no freight to the spirit-shore."
  Was the captain's grim reply;
The wild waves echoed it back with a roar,
  And the rich man heaved a sigh;
"Our orders are strict, from the King Supreme
That nothing of earth must cross the stream."

"O, what shall I do in that far-off land!"
  Cried the rich man in despair;
Though my mansions here are large and grand,
  I am homeless and friendless there:
Oh, carry my gold to the further shore!"
His voice was lost in the wild waves' roar.

They ferried the rich man's soul across—
  They buried his body cold;
The friends behind little felt his loss
  As they stood 'mid his bags of gold;
They wiped from their eyes a few false tears,
Then quarreled and fought o'er his wealth for years.

Another man came to the river side;
  And he walked with a steady tread
For he carried no gold-bags, closely tied—
  He had often begged for bread;
But he gazed with joy on the rolling stream—
For his dearest friend was the King Supreme.

And others came down to say farewell
  As he parted away from earth;
They wept when they heard the tolling bell,
  For long had they known his worth;
With loving deeds for his golden pen
He had written his name on the hearts of men.

They ferried his soul across the stream,
  They buried his body cold;
And he found a home with the King Supreme
  In the mansions built of gold;
Though he lived on earth, 'mid its care and strife
He had also lived for the better life.

LAUGHING EYES—A LOVE SONG.

TALK to me with your laughing eyes,
    And tell me love's bewitching tale;
  Clear as the depths of summer skies
    Thine eyes can hearts of stone assail;
  'Neath them emotions, pure, arise,
Like blossoms sweet o'er hill and dale—
Talk to me with your laughing eyes
  And tell me love's bewitching tale.

Chorus.

Sparkling and bright with love's sweet light,
Talk to me with your laughing eyes.

There is a language that the tongue
  Can seldom speak, though oft it try:
It stammers and is soon unstrung
  While love's sweet words grow faint and die;

Clear as the depths of summer skies,
  The eye can speak, though tongue may fail;
Talk to me with your laughing eyes,
  And tell me love's bewitching tale.

Eyes are the windows of the soul,
  In hoary age and blooming youth;
While life's short years swift by us roll,
  O, let them shine with love and truth;
Tell me, sweet love, must I arise
  And leave this place lit up by thine,
Without a glance from those dear eyes
  To tell me that your heart is mine?

A LITTLE SUMMER ALL SHUT IN.

'TIS sweet to have, when the storms begin
    To roam o'er the earth so wide,
  A little summer, all shut in
    From the frozen world outside;
  A little summer, all our own,
From the days when the robins go,
To the days when they come from a warmer zone,
  And the Pansies peep from the snow.

The rich may daily on dainties dine,
  And daily on velvet tread,
But give to my home the trailing vine,
  And the blooming flowers instead;
A cheerful wife, in a sunny room,
  Who sings as she flits about;
What care I, then, with the plants in bloom,
  For the wintry winds without.

How sweet to come from the constant din
   Of life's contending tide,
To my little summer, all shut in,
   From the frozen world outside;
To watch the bright geraniums grow,
   From the bud to the opening flower,
While the outer world lies under the snow,
And bound by the Ice King's power.

The poet sings of the better land,
   "Where flowers immortal bloom."
And so I can partly understand
   The glories beyond the tomb;
How sad and dreary this earth would be,
   Trough all of the weary hours,
Had God not given to you and me
   The beautiful birds and flowers.

THE LESSON OF THE LILIES.

I 'LL tell to thee the story of the Christ born o'er the
   sea;
His followers were all poor men from stormy Galilee,
And, yet, they left their fishing nets, with which they
   gained their bread,
To follow him who had not where to lay his weary head.

They stood once in an open field where lilies, pure, did
   grow;
And o'er their heads the swift-winged birds were flying
   to and fro;

Christ told them of his Father's love—his Father's constant care,
And proved it by the lilies and the commoners of air.

"Behold," he said, "the birds above! they neither sow
nor reap;
They gather up no golden grain, in spacious barns to
keep;
And, yet, your Father feedeth them, and guides them on
their way,
Shall He not feed His children, who are dearer, far,
than they?

"Consider, thou, the lilies! They toil not, neither spin,
Yet Solomon in rich array could not with them begin;
If God so clothe the fading grass that must tomorrow die,
He surely will bow down His ear to hear thy faintest cry.

Then lift your head, desponding man! There is a hand
to guide!
There is a Great Provider who, surely, will provide;
Let this lesson come with comfort to thy little ones and
thee—
This lesson of the lilies from the land far o'er the sea.

❧

A MEMORIAL POEM.

IN MEMORY OF HATTIE ACKER FRIEDLEY.

WE'LL garland her casket with beautiful flowers,
And weep for the loved one we'll ne'er see
again,
Her sweet spirit fled when the Autumn leaf
showers

Were falling on woodland, and mountain and glen.
The light of her smile has gone out of the dwelling—
　The home that her faithful hands tended with care;
With anguish untold many hearts are now swelling,
　For lost is the beautiful jewel so rare.

The Autumn leaves fall on the upland and meadow,
　The flowers have faded from paths where we roam,
And like them she fell, and bereavement's dark shadow
　Now rests on the bright little circle at home.
Her beautiful life was a joy and a blessing
　To all who came into the light of her love;
Her nearest and dearest will miss her caressing
　And sigh for the one in the mansions above.

The summer shall come, when the storms have departed;
　The earth shall again yield the beautiful flowers;
But she whom we loved, who was so tender hearted,
　Shall gladden, O never, this earth life of ours;
But Faith lifts her eyes and looks over the river,
　And sees through the tear-mist the Beautiful Shore,
Where hearts are united and Death cometh never,
　And sickness, and sorrow, and sighing are o'er.

A shining path leads to the life she is living;
　Let us strive for the rest she has entered at last:
Let us give forth the light that her life lamp was giving,
　And meet her when Time's stormy billows are past.
Then with her we'll share in the life everlasting,
　The bliss that the Father prepares for His own;
Where love's fairest blossoms shall never know blasting,
　And shadows ne'er darken the light of His throne.

OUR ANCIENT LANDMARK.

A DEDICATION POEM.

Read at Batavia, N. Y., October 14, 1894, before President Cleveland's cabinet at the dedication of the Old Land Office of the Holland Purchase built about the year 1804, bought in 1894 by the Holland Purchase Historical Society and dedicated by John G. Carlisle, Secretary of the Treasury of the United States, as a memorial to Robert Morris, the great Superintendent of Finance of the United States during the Revolution, and the first owner of the lands in Western New York.

WHEN to the banks of Jordan's rolling tide
   The hosts of God from far off Egypt came—
With cloudy pillar their long march to guide,
   Past Sinai's awful mount of smoke and flame,

They found no passage the dark waters o'er,
   No way to cross the overflowing stream,
And Israel's warriors stood upon the shore
   But could not reach the Canaan of their dream.

Then Joshua, their leader, strong and true,
   Lifted his voice and soul to God in prayer,
While angel hands the billows backward threw,
   And made a passage for God's people there.

The ark of God moved on at His command,
   And forward moved the host o'er Jordan's bed;
Their feet as dry as when, through burning sand,
   Their weary way the cloudy pillar led.

Then reared they high a monument of stones,
  To tell to generations yet unborn
How he, the King of Kings, on throne of thrones,
  Held back the waters on that glorious morn.

In after years, when sunny youth inquired
  "What mean these stones?" the gray haired fathers told
The story that again their bosoms fired,
  The story of deliv'rances of old.

  *   *   *   *   *   *   *   *   *

Before us stands this monument of ours,
  That hath these many years the storms withstood;
Reared 'mid the perfumes of the forest flowers,
  In shadows cast by monarchs of the wood.

Reared on the banks of Tonawanda's stream,
  Which, fed by living springs and rippling rills,
Winds down the vale as gentle as a dream,
  From the blue domes of the Wyoming hills.

Reared at the junction of two Indian trails,
  Where chieftains met to seal some white man's doom;
While war cries mingled with the night wind's wails
  And council fires lit up the forest's gloom.

Today when sunny youth of us inquires
  "What mean these stones?" we stop with pride to tell
Of wonders wrought by high Ambition's fires,
  And honest toil, o'er every hill and dell.

As sea shells sing forever of the sea,
  Though borne inland a thousand miles away,
So do these walls give forth to you and me
  The sounds and songs of our forefathers' day.

I hear the echo of the woodman's stroke
  Resounding through the aisles of forest gray;
The crash of giant elm and sturdy oak,
  As they for towns and fertile fields make way.

I hear the stage horn's blast at close of day,
  The wheels that rumble o'er the rugged road,
While feeding deer affrighted speed away,
  To tangled thickets of their wild abode.

I hear the postman as he hastens here
  From forest op'nings, where the blue smoke curled,
O'er winding pathways, desolate and drear,
  Where now are beaten highways of the world.

The breaking twigs in thicket dense I hear,
  Where stealthy panther creeps upon his prey;
The victim's struggle and his cries of fear,
  Which fainter grow, and die, at last, away.

I hear the whirring of the spinning wheel,
  The crackling of the logs on fireplace bright,
The scythe-stone grinding on the blade of steel,
  The owl complaining through the lonely night.

I hear the merriments of olden times,
  The apple parings and the husking bees;
The laughter ringing out like merry chimes
  From rustic haunts beneath the forest trees.

What mean these stones?" They tell of honest men,
  Who lived and loved in years now flown away,
Who toiled for us with hammer, plow and pen,
  From rosy morn until the evening gray.

Their grandest castles, builded in the air,
  When they at noon sought rest in shady dell,
Were not, though fancy painted, half so fair
  As these in which their children's children dwell.

We now enjoy the fruitage of their toil,
  From where the Genesee's bright waters flow,
To where Niag'ra's billows in turmoil
  Plunge o'er the precipice to depths below.

All honor to those noble men who laid
  The firm foundation of our wealth and pride!
They rest today beneath the maple's shade,
  All undisturbed by traffic's surging tide.

O could they wake from slumber of the tomb,
  What changes would they note beneath these skies!
A wilderness transformed to Eden bloom,
  With wonders everywhere to greet their eyes.

What though their forms have crumbled into dust,
  Their deeds shall shine resplendent as the sun;
What though their plowshares are consumed by rust,
  The work they wrought will never be undone.

All honor to that man who forward came
  In "times that tried men's souls," long years ago,
And gave his wealth and pledged his spotless name,
  To drive forever from our shores the foe.

The memory of Morris long shall stand,
  With honor crowned beneath these sunny skies;
The sons and daughters of our favored land
  Will not forget his love and sacrifice.

'Twas he who wakened from their wild repose
These hills and valleys, stretching far away,
That now unfold their beauty like the rose
That gives its dew drops to the kiss of Day.

When armies faltered for the lack of bread,
When bugles ceased to call and drums to beat,
He came with patriot heart and hasty tread,
And laid his millions at his country's feet.

Freedom's immortal Declaration bears
The name of Morris on its sacred page;
With changing years his record brighter wears,
While granite crumbles at the touch of Age.

Then dedicate this structure to his name,
While music sweet floats out upon the air.
These walls shall to the world speak forth his fame,
And these fair valleys shall be still more fair.

* * * * * * * * *

As sea shells sing forever of the sea,
Bear them away from ocean where thou wilt,
So shall ye sing, O walls, through years to be,
Of great success on firm foundation built.

The storms and tempests of the rolling years
Have beat thy granite walls by night and day,
Yet thou hast stood, amid man's hopes and fears,
To see the hands that made thee mould away.

Thou shalt remain to bid this land rejoice,
Till these fair youths who gaze upon thee now
Shall speak thy praises with a trembling voice,
When hoary hairs adorn each wrinkled brow.

The waves of progress which have swept away
  Thy brother landmarks, built of wood or stone,
Broke at thy feet and vanished into spray,
  And left thee, gray old monarch, here—alone.

"A thing of beauty" thou has always stood,
  "A thing of beauty" thou shalt ever stand,
At first the glory of the lonely wood,
  But now the glory of the teeming land.

Sing on, O walls, though years their changes bring,
  Sing on while all the bells of progress chime,
Sing of the past, of future glory sing,
  While thy quaint form defies the march of time!

MY HEARTH AND HOME.

THEY are telling of islands where sweet flowers
    bloom,
    And where streams flow o'er bright sands of
    gold;
    Where the years roll around with eternal perfume
From the blossoms that richly unfold;
Let them wander, who will, 'neath those bright, sunny
  skies,
  Let them gather the gold as they roam,
I have treasures more precious, with love-beaming eyes
  In my bright little circle at home.

I have flowers more fair than the rare ones that bloom
  On those islands at rest in the seas;
And their love is more precious to me than perfume
  Borne away on the wings of the breeze;

Oh! I know that the song of the warbler is sweet
  In the beautiful isles o'er the foam;
But be mine the sweet music of dear little feet
  As we meet at the threshold of home.

Oh! how sweet when the day, with its labor, is o'er,
  To away from its clamor and din,
And rejoice as I shut the world out at the door
  O'er my dear little kingdom within;
To be met by bright eyes looking love into mine
  And sweet lips lifted up for a kiss,
Then to feel the soft arms that around me entwine
  Makes my home a sweet Eden of bliss.

There are those on life's way who are drifting along
  The wild sport of the winds and the foam;
They will sigh, as they list to the words of my song,
  For the blessed endearments of home;
I will give, then, the praise to my Father above
  For the joys that around me arise,
And look forward, and hope to be brought by His love
  To a beautiful home in the skies.

SWEET BLOSSOM OF THE LONELY WOOD.

SWEET blossom of the lonely wood,
  Why waste thy sweets in solitude?
  'Mid scenes so desolate, and rude.

Companion, thou, of tangled weeds,
That shower down their deadly seeds
Where serpents creep, among the reeds.

A queen art thou, upon a throne
That sparkles, with the moss o'ergrown;
A queen, but oh! why reign alone?

Thy beauty would adorn the bowers,
Where fair ones spend the summer hours,
And kiss the blush from poorer flowers.

Ah! now I know, God placed thee here
Amid this desolation, drear;
Not thine to question, thine to cheer.

A lesson thou hast taught today;
Though lonely be the Christian's way,
'Tis his to toil, and his to pray.

Not always in the highest place
Are those who see God's smiling face,
And feel the visits of His grace.

God hath a smile for all the good;
For those who bloom in solitude
Like thee, sweet blossom of the wood.

※

SANTA CLAUS.

HE comes in the night! He comes in the night!
  He softly, silently comes;
When the little brown heads, on their pillows so
    white,
  Are dreaming of bugles and drums;

He cuts through the snow, like a ship through the foam,
 While the white flakes around him whirl;
Who tells him? I know not; he findeth the home
 Of each good little boy and girl.

IIis sleigh it is long, and deep, and wide;
 It will carry a host of things;
While dozens of drums hang 'round, on the side,
 With the sticks sticking under the strings;
And yet not the sound of a drum is heard—
 Not a bugle blast is blown—
As he mounts to the chimney-tops like a bird
 And pops down in like a stone.

The little red stockings he silently fills,
 Till the stockings will hold no more;
The bright little sleds, for the great snow hills,
 Are quickly let down to the floor;
Then Santa Claus mounts to the roof like a bird,
 And glides to the seat in his sleigh;
Not the sound of a bugle or drum is heard,
 As he noiselessly moves away.

He rides to the west; he rides to the east;
 Of his goodies he touches not one;
He eateth the crums of the Christmas feast,
 When the dear little folks are done;
Old Santa Claus doeth what good he can
 This beautiful mission is his—
Then, children, be good to the little old man
 When you find who the little man is.

A TALK WITH ROBIN REDBREAST.

GOOD morning, robin redbreast,
　　Come in and toast your toes!
You cannot warm them 'neath your vest,
　　Though like the fire it glows,
　　Come in, come in, my pretty bird,
You're here, I fear too soon,
No leaves are by the breezes stirred,
　　The sun is cold at noon.

Pray tell me, robin redbreast,
　　What made you hurry so
To leave the sunny southern land
　　For northern ice and snow?
You studied "Probabilities"
　　And now are filled with aches?
They told you it was sunny
　　Around the "lower lakes."

Poor little robin redbreast,
　　The sun may brightly shine
And yet the bitter biting blast
　　May chill that form of thine;
Like friends who smile upon me
　　With no love in their hearts,
I'm surely none the poorer
　　When the chilling smile departs.

Be patient robin redbreast;
  Now make the most of it;
Just put the best foot forward;
  From ground to tree-top flit.
Keep flying 'round—keep singing,
  Though cold may be the hours,
The days to come are bringing
  The perfume of the flowers.

❧

SCHOOL IS OUT TODAY.

SEW up his breeches, Nancy! and sew 'em good
    and stout!
  Despite the patches, and the thread, his knees will
    soon be out.
  The stickin' salve and arnica, so snugly stowed
    away,
Get out, and have 'em handy, for school is out today.

It isn't to be wondered at that you will need sich things
When boys try flyin' from the barn, and find they haven't
    wings:
Or when they scale the fences and shaky boards give way,
And homeward come the wounded like soldiers from the
    fray.

Take all your silver trinkets, and trinkets made of gold,
And hide 'em as a shepherd hides his sheep within the
    fold;
Or they will waste their glitter in the long and tangled
    grass,
In some forsaken corner, where but seldom mortals pass.

As the farmers fix for winter, when the winter draweth
    near—
As the sailors trim for battle, and the decks for action
    clear—
As men arrange their business when they wish to go away
So set your house in order, for school is out today.

Soon the shouts of all the children in and out the house
    will ring;
Soon your clothes line will be hangin' on the maple for a
    swing:
And my tools, now in their places, one by one away will
    roam,
Then I'll wish the boys in Halifax—if Halifax is home.

As the songsters shed their feathers, John has shed his
    boots today
And barefoot in the clover he is hiving bees away,
If I ain't much mistaken—if he keeps to work at that
He'll find that he has got one that isn't in his hat.

Then I guess you'll need your arnica, your stickin' salve,
    and sich
For a sting that striketh deeper than the hardest master's
    switch;
Then I guess John will remember, as he seeks for other
    joys,
That bees delight in liberty as well as barefoot boys.

Ah! wife another school is out—the one across the way;
I saw crape hangin' on the door when I came by today,
Her lessons in affliction, in suffering and pain,
Were hard, but, then, the school for her will ne'er be
    called again.

Thus, one by one, we're comin' to the long vacation time,
When we'll sport amid the flowers of that bright, eternal
  clime
If we're on the roll of honor, if we get the blest award
At the great examination, the judgment of the Lord.

*

INDEPENDENCE DAY.

ALL hail this glad day! In the years flown away
          Our forefathers fought,
      And with their red blood our inheritance bought;
      The merry bells chime; we have journeyed thro'
          time
              Till again we all cheer
For this, the great day of our national year.
Oh, chime the sweet bells from the sea to the sea
For the land of the brave and the home of the free!
    Now, backward the eyes of the Nation are turning—
      Now, proudly we sing of old victories won,
    In backwoodman's cottage, in great halls of learning
      We tell of the deeds the forefathers have done.
Oh, chime the sweet bells from the sea to the sea,
For the home of the brave and the land of the free!

We are brushing the dust and a century's must
          From the records of old—
The records more precious than silver and gold;
With eyes all aglow, we read how the foe
          Fled away o'er the sod,
From men with dry powder, and great faith in God.

The drums of the forefathers, hearest them beating,
   Where farmers and workmen have shouldered their
     guns?
   Like a horse for the race they there chafe for the
     meeting
   With their strong oppressors—Britannia's proud sons,
Let the merry bells chime from the sea to the sea
While we talk of the brave men who fought to be free.

The eyes of the world, on our banner unfurled,
     Are gazing today,
Amazed at the brightness that maketh our way;
It seemeth a dream; let the proud eagle scream
     From the mountain crag, bold,
For our country, whose glories can never be told:
    Float out, starry flag, 'mong the flags of each nation,
     From vessels that rest in the ports of the world;
    For God set thy stars, thou art His great creation—
     Thou banner of banners wherever unfurled.
Let the merry bells chime from the sea to the sea,
While we sing of our banner—the flag of the free.

When the battle-smoke 'rose, from the guns of our foes,
     On the plains of the South,
Our brave boys marched up to the hot cannon's mouth;
There they cried, "We will fight for God and the Right,
     Till we weave from the clouds
Bright crowns for our heroes, for traitors—their shrouds'!
    The battle is over; the Peace-Angel reigneth
     From mountains of inland to storm-traversed sea;
    Not a slave in the land in his fetters remaineth
     To mock at our song when we sing we are free—
Let the merry bells chime, on this glorious day,
For united, again, are the blue and the gray.

All hail this glad day! We have come from the fray—
    From the blood, and the tears,
To the glory that crowns more than one hundred years;
United we stand, in this, our bright land;
    By the blood of the slain,
We swear that united we'll ever remain.
    Let never a man—if suspected of treason—
    Be lifted to places of honor and trust;
    From war's desolation, Oh! rest for a season,
    And let the bright bayonet gather its rust.
Chime on the sweet bells in the towers, my boys!
The boom of the cannon is only for noise.

All hail this glad day! In the lands far away
    The American born
May be pardoned their pride on this glorious morn;
For the nations of earth—gray with age at our birth—
    Will join in the cheer
That shall ring 'round the world this glad day of the year.
    The oppressed of all lands who now groan in oppres-
        sion
    Shall gaze with new hopes to the Star of West;
    They will sigh for the blessings that flee their pos-
        session—
    The blessings with which we so richly are blest.
Americans, chime the sweet bells o'er the sea,
And sing of your home in the land of the free.

All glory to God , who hath broken the rod
    Of Oppression and Wrong—
Who spares us to sing, now, our National Song;
    Who makes us to be
The home of the brave and the land of the free,

May he not forsake the great vine of his planting;
　　May we not depart from our forefather's God;
His praise let America ever be chanting,
　　That freedom forever may bloom on our sod.
Oh! chime the sweet bells from the sea to the sea,
For the home of the brave and the land of the free!

&

SCHOOL BEGINS TODAY.

'M glad vacation's over, and school is called again!
For thirteen weeks my romping boys have crazed their
　　　mother's brain;
For thirteen weeks I've counted the sultry days away:
I'm glad vacation's over and school begins today.

They say that teachers cannot teach—that scholars can-
　　not learn
Thro' all the days of summer—the days that fairly burn;
I wonder if they ever ask how mothers get along
With romping boys who find their joys in doing some-
　　thing wrong?

There's John and Joe, and Jimmy, their clothes were
　　nearly new
When they came home from school that day and said the
　　term was through;
Now John, and Joe, and Jimmy, with sun-brown hands
　　and feet
Come in at night in 'bout the plight of beggars on the
　　street!

There is no order in the house; I cannot find a thing;
The drawers are tumbled upside down with six hands
    hunting string;
The chairs are always in a row—the whole house fairly
    jars
With Jimmy jumping off and on to run his train of cars.

My brand-new carving-knife I found out in the grass,
    where Joe
Had used it making arrows for Jimmy's little bow;
And John came home from fishing—came whistling
    through the gate—
With father's best tobacco-box filled up with worms for
    bait.

The bees have had a frightful time the whole vacation
    through;
They could not hide a nest away the best that they could
    do.
I heard the rooster crow this morn, to me he seemed to say
"I'm glad vacation's over and school begins today!"

"All work" they say "without some play makes Jack a
    stupid boy;
Well that's a good old adage and gives the urchins joy;
But if that man who wrote it lived now and owned a son
He'd sit up late and scratch his pate to write a different
    one.

There, there, I'm not complaining! Though weary of
    the noise;
I love, as only mothers can, my rat'ling, romping boys.

And I shall watch for four o'clock through every coming
    day,
When I can see my darlings out in the yard at play.

I've one dear boy now sleeping beneath the summer sod,
He took a long vacation when he went home to God!
When life's rough school is over I'll meet him by and bye
Where graves ne'er hide our treasures—where dear ones
    never die.

AUTUMN.

OH, Tom my friend, 'tis autumn!   Don't you see
    The faded blossoms bow their heads and die?
There, hear the apples falling from the tree,
    As friends are falling, near to you and I.

See yonder man with cider apples pass,
    A heavy load for that poor horse to draw;
Tom! will you drink your cider from a glass?
    To me 'tis sweeter coming through a straw.

Let's drink it now—'tis sweet, my dear old friend,
    Let's drink it now—'t is harmless apple-juice.
For if we wait 'twill set us up on end
    And make us to our friends of little use

The chestnut burrs Jack Frost has opened wide;
    There go the boys, a nutting, to the wood!
When winter winds sweep by the bright fireside
    The chestnuts and the butternuts are good.

Long years ago—before we grew to men—
  Those tangled bushes oft we've traveled through;
The woods are smaller now than they were then;
  The circle of old friends is smaller, too.

The huskers labor well in yonder field;
  Another husker on the fence doth rest;
The hollow in that tree would some corn yield;
  Wise squirrel, he, to store with food his nest.

How is it, Tom, with you and I today?
  Our autumn neareth, with its toil and strife;
Have we been wise and treasures laid away,
  To be enjoyed in the hereafter life?

*

SEPTEMBER BELLS.

SEPTEMBER bells are ringing o'er all the beautious
      land—
  In little country school-house and college, large
      and grand;
    September bells are ringing, and this is what they say:
Come in! Vacation's ended, and school begins today.

Come in from shaded waters of rivers broad, and lake!
Put up your fishing-tackle, and pen and pencil take!
The time has come for study, the time is o'er for play;
September bells are ringing, and school begins today!

Come from the shady bowers where the cool breeze fans
      the brow;
Come with your sun-brown faces and o'er knotty problems
      bow:

Brush the dust from the worn grammar, reading-book
and algebra;
September bells are ringing, and school begins today!

"Life is real, life is earnest," we must work as well as play;
We must leave the shady foot-path for the broad and
dusty way;
With our minds and bodies rested, by the waters bright
and cool;
Now September bells are ringing let us hasten back to
school.

Ah, how many backs, a-weary, never loose the heavy load!
Ah, how many feet, so dusty, never find a shady road!
They may hear of others resting, where the wild waves
break in spray;
But their task is never ended—comes for them no time
for play.

Streams may flow with charming music through the
forests wide and still,
But they only hear the clatter of the shop or dusty mill;
Breezes cool may fan the faces of the few in shady bowers,
While the millions keep their places, at their tasks,
through sultry hours.

Go not back, then, to your studies, grieving o'er vacation past;
Fast your feet fled to the woodlands, let them speed to
the school as fast;
Think of thousands upon thousands who on play-grounds
ne'er appear—
Whose September bells for toiling ring through all the
weary year.

NEW YEAR THOUGHTS.

NOW our life boat plows the billows
   Past the fast receding years;
  Friends we lay beneath the willows
   While we weep bereavement's tears;
All in vain our fond heart's yearning
  For the loving friends of yore;
Only memory's lights are burning
  On the dead year's phantom shore.

We have sailed past golden hours
  In which good we might have done;
But we sat amid the flowers
  Basking in the summer sun:
All in vain our hearts are yearning,
  Back those hours can come no more:
Only memory's lights are burning
  On the dead year's phantom shore.

Hasty words our lips have spoken—
  Words we gladly would recall—
But the golden bowl is broken,
  On our hearts there rests a pall:
All in vain our hearts are yearning
  For the trusting love of yore;
Only memory's lights are burning
  On the dead year's phantom shore.

Or, perhaps, a promise given,
  We have failed to watch and keep;
Now a cloud o'erspreadeth heaven
  And our heads are bowed to weep;
By the past a lesson learning
  Keep thy word forever more;
Then shall brighter lights be burning
  On the dead year's phantom shore.

If to help the poor and needy
  We a willing hand have given,
Our reward may not be speedy—
  May not reach us this side heaven;—
For it let us not be yearning—
  It is waiting on before—
While behind us brightly burning,
  Memory's lights illume the shore.

Let us seize the golden present;
  This is ours, and only this;
Make the fleeting moments pleasant
  With the deeds that bring us bliss:
Then our hearts will not be yearning
  For the years that come no more;
Then shall hope's bright lights be burning —
  On the nearing Spirit shore.

THE ISLES OF THE YEARS.

WHAT a mystical stream is the river of Time
  As it flows to Eternity's sea;
The voyage of the good is a voyage sublime,
As he steers his boat to a brighter clime
  With the pure and the blest to be.

The mist never lifts from the stream before
    To tell us of joy or pain;
At the dip of the boatman's dripping oar
It rises to show us the parallel shore,
    Then kisses the wave again.

What a mystical boat is this body of ours
    That ferries the soul along
By the piercing thorns, and the blooming flowers,
Past barren shores and inviting bowers,
    To the kingdom of angel song.

The years come like isles in a dreamer's dream,
    As we glide down the stream of Time;
Oh! isles of my childhood, how beauteous ye seem!
In the wake of my boat ye rise from the stream
    A mirage on clouds sublime!

The islands of youth—the enchanted isles—
    How sluggish the stream moves by;
The summer sun on the landscape smiles,
The bud and the blossom the soul beguiles,
    And the song-larks mount the sky.

Isles of our manhood! Swifter flows
    The stream; and it breaks in spray;
The drooping blossoms the thorns disclose;
Dark clouds of care—some black with woes—
    O'ershadows the boatman's way.

Isles of old age—Oh! barren isles!
    Oh! bleak and desolate shores!
If a life well spent on the boatman smiles,
He dreams of home the remaining miles,
    Then peacefully drops the oars,

While all unseen by mortal eye
    The angel pilots come,
And swift to the isle of the "By-and-By"—
Somewhere 'neath Eternity's cloudless sky
    The soul finds its God and home.

&

FATHER TIME AND THE NEWSBOY.

I 'M a rosy-cheeked boy, knowing little of life;
Its cares do not burden, nor vex me its strife;
My pleasures are simple, my sorrows are few,
They come, and are gone, like the pearl-drops of dew;
My life is before me—a wide swelling tide—
Not much of it tested, nor much of it tried;
My years are like snails, creeping, down at my feet,
And I wonder how old men can call them so fleet;
In summer, when bees in the blossoms do hum,
It seems as though Christmas-time never would come;
And, then, in the winter, when snow flakes do fly,
It seems like an age to the Fourth of July.

With my heart like a feather—my cheeks all aglow—
I want everything, all around me, to go;
My top it must spin, and my kite it must fly,
'Til it looks like a bird far away in the sky;
When I go on an errand, or searching for fun,
No walking for me, sir, I'm off on a run.

I met Father Time, in my rambles, one day,
His form it was bent and his hairs they were gray;
He carried a sharp-cutting scythe in his hand,
To mow down all people, in every land;

I knew he was wise, for, about every day,
"Time will tell," I do hear all the big people say;
He must be so strong, for when things are in doubt
I hear the men say "time will bring it about;"
I've read it in prose, and I've read it in rhyme,
All the great things of earth are accomplished by time.
Then I took a look at him, all crippled and bent,
And wondered; then up a step nearer I went;
"Dear father," I said, "I would much like to know,
How you do so much work when you travel so slow."

"My bright little fellow," old Father Time said,
"I know all the thoughts that do bother your head;
Take a journey with me and I'll show, if I can
Though I'm slow to the boy, I am fast to the man."
Then he led me away to a weaver's low room,
Where he sat hard at work by a dusty old loom;
With a rattle-te-bang, up and down went his feet,
'Til I thought the old thing all to pieces he'd beat;
Then a stick, wound with string, back and forth he let fly,
Like a flash of the lightning that shoots from the sky.
"That stick is a shuttle," old Father Time said;
"Thus my years fly away o'er the agéd man's head."

"My days are swifter than a weaver's shuttle."—Job. 7:6.

Then we wandered away from the weaver's low room
To the hills and the meadows, all covered with bloom;
The sun shone so bright, and a warm southern breeze
Blew so strong, that it bowed low the tops of the trees;
A white cloud came sailing along through the sky
And, soon, its great shadow went rapidly by;
"My dear little fellow," Time smilingly said,
"My days fly like that o'er the agéd man's head."

" Man is like to vanity; his days are as a shadow that passeth away."—David.

Then we came to a mount; there we stopped on our way
And rested all night, 'til the break of the day:
Then I looked, and a vapor hid all things below,
Though the bells could be heard as they swung to and fro;
I gazed 'til the sun rising out of the east
Smiled down on the earth like a host at a feast.
Soon the vapor was gone, and the valley, so green,
Far below, at my feet in its beauty was seen.
"As vapors do vanish," Time smilingly said,
"Thus my years fly away o'er the agéd man's head."

" For what is your life? It is even a vapor that appear-
eth for a little time and then vanisheth away."—James.

Down the mountain we sped—for I found Time could fly—
'Til we came to the meadows once gay to the eye;
But their glory had flown, they could charm me no more,
For the reapers had been there the evening before;
The long waving grass, and the blossoms, so sweet,
Together were withered, and dead at my feet;
Time pointed his finger, as on we did pass,
And whispered, low, to me, "all flesh is but grass."

" For all flesh is as grass, and all the glory of man as the
flower of grass.   The grass withereth and the flower thereof
falleth away."—I Peter, 1-24.

"My bright little fellow," Time then said to me,
"I must keep at my work, on the land and the sea;
I've taught you a lesson with shadows and flowers
I trust you'll remember through all of life's hours;

'Time flies,' has been written in many a book,
And spoken in many a lover's fond look;
Time flies to the miser, who hoards up his gold;
Time flies to the thousands, who feel they grow old;
Time flies, my dear boy, do not idle away
A year that I give you, not even a day;
My moments are golden, my worth better known
When days they have vanished, and years they have flown;
You thought me as slow as the snails at your feet,
The roe on the mountains was never more fleet;
Then mind what I teach you, and when you are old
Your wealth none shall reckon with silver and gold;
My dear little boy, I must now disappear,
I'll try hard to bring you a happy New Year."

Time was gone like a flash, and by looking about
I saw it was time to be taking my route;
The things that were taught me, can older boys bless,
So I send them to all in my yearly address;
I wish all my patrons and every dear friend,
A happy New Year, from beginning to end

—CARRIER BOY.

***

JOE BROWN'S DEFEAT.

SOME men take to a horse;
Some to a dog and gun,
While others, rather than stand and fight,
Will take to their heels and run;
In the latter, very numerous class,
Tom Tinkham numbered one.

Tom was a muscular man,
Yet he did not think it right
To practice the art of self-defense
To protect himself in a fight;
So he quietly lived, the first for peace,
And in war, the first—for flight.

Joe Brown was a different man—
A neighbor of Tom's, and rough—
In all the town and country through
He was called by the "fancy," tough.
He talked very loud, and so, of course,
He played well the game of "bluff."

Wherever a fair was held,
Joe Brown was the foremost there;
His boots kicking hard at somebody's shins,
His hands in somebody's hair.
The words of his mouth were always foul,
And all of his tricks unfair.

His victories made him bold—
He never had known defeat—
Till he got to be troublesome everywhere,
And insolent on the street;
And good people prayed that this evil man
Something more than his match might meet.

Though talented we may be—
Though we win for ourselves renown—
There is always a better man somewhere
Who will take from our heads the crown,
And bring all our pride and self-conceit,
Like a used-up rocket, down.

The good people's prayers were heard,
For Joe found his match one day,
When he got Tom Tinkham cornered up
Where he could not run away;
Tom went for Joe like a hurricane,
And the good people ceased to pray.

When he got off from his bed
His lips wore a sullen pout;
When he met the boys on the street, he said—
As he limped with his cane about—
"You can't always tell what there is in a man
Till necessity brings it out."

*

JOHNNIE McGUIRE'S RIDE.

(In the New York State Institution for the Blind at Batavia
there was a blind and cripple boy named Johnnie McGuire, from
Troy, N. Y. A short time ago the other pupils bought a cart for
him with the money they had saved for that purpose. Now,
when the weather is pleasant, Johnnie may be seen riding out into
the country for apples, with two blind boys for his team.)

POETS have sung of Sheridan—
Sung of the horse, and valiant man;
Now let an humbler one aspire
To sing of the ride of Johnnie McGuire.
Back from the wars the kings of old
Rode in their chariots rich with gold,
While thousands shouted, 'mid beating drums,
"He comes—the conquering hero comes!"

Back of the glitter of gold and spear
Those proud kings rode with a look severe;
For under the armor that brightly shone
They carried a heart as hard as stone;
Over the dying and dead their ride
Was one of cruel power and pride.
Down through the crowded thoroughfare
Rideth a haughty millionaire;
Over the pavements the horses prance;
On trimmings of silver the sunbeams dance.
What careth he, in the rolling coach,
That winter, and want, doth the poor approach?
Over the pavement his is a ride,
With every earth-want satisfied.
Over the sod, through smoke and flame,
A soldier rideth to win a name;
Missiles of death fly thick and fast
And strong men fall as his form goes past;
The groans of the dying—the crimson tide
Telleth the tale of a soldier's ride.

    *   *   *   *   *   *   *   *   *

"Pass in the pennies, boys, one by one!
The work of collecting has now begun.
Pass in the pennies with cheerful heart
And Johnnie McGuire shall ride in a cart!
Johnnie's a cripple, while we are strong:
In a nice new cart we can take him along
When to the country the roads we tread
For Golden Pippins and Baldwins red."
Thus said the blind boys one to another,
Prompted by love for a crippled brother;
The pennies were given with great delight,
As the widow of old gave in her mite.

Oh! beautiful Indian summer day,
When the soft south winds play hide-and-seek:
Brushing the maiden's tresses away
From the rose that blooms on her fair young cheek;
What though the blind boys cannot see
The golden leaves on the maple tree?
What though forever are closed their eyes
To the green of the earth and the blue of the skies?
Into their hearts doth the glory steal,
For what we see it is theirs to feel.

Oh! smooth, white roads stretching far away
Into the country from out the town!
Where, all through the night and live long day
The golden apples come thumping down,
What roads for a lordly millionaire
To traverse in pride, with a haughty air!
What smooth white roads for a good long race
By the merry boys with sun-brown face!

Did you hear that rattle and merry shout?
That's John McGuire, sir, driving out.
See how he sits in his brand new cart,
Proud as a king—with a happier heart—
Where is he going? out of the town
Where golden apples come thumping down.
Over the hill they have disappeared
To the fields where the frosts have the grasses seared,
Soon they will shout 'neath the apple trees,
Happy as kings, and busy as bees
They'll eat what they want and afterwards store,
All around Johnnie, a peck or more;
Then with a shout and a crack of the whip
Off they will start on their homeward trip.

Happy are they who draw the load,
Feeling their way on the long bright road;
Happy is he who rides in the cart,
Sightless his eyes but merry his heart;
Thousands of people who see today
Are more unfortunate, far, than they.

Up through the broad, smooth avenue
　　There they come with their golden store!
Each to the other is kind and true,
　　May they remain so till life is o'er.

Not as the powerful kings of old
Rode in their chariots rich with gold;
Not as the worldly millionaire
Down through the crowded thoroughfare;
Not as the soldier who seeks to destroy,
Rideth that blind and crippled boy:
And yet who is there that dare to say
That angels have not looked down today
From rolling chariot of unseen fire
On the homelier ride of Johnnie McGuire.

❧

TOM CARRINGTON—A TRUE TALE OF ENGLAND.

"IN England lived Tom Carrington,
Who vowed that he would never run
For living man or haunting ghost;
Whose bravery was all his boast.

Tom's face was marked by many scars,
Received in hard-fought British wars;
No sight by day nor evening dim
He said could ever frighten him.

In life-paths trod by mortal feet,
Greatest extremes do often meet,
And meeting, they in friendship tarry,
'Till at the last they love and marry.

Thus men, more savage far than knives,
Wed patient, tender-hearted wives;
And scolding women—'tis no joke—
Wed men the devil can't provoke.

'Twas thus with Tom! though he was brave,
His wife was to her fears a slave:
By day she saw some sign of evil,
By night she dreamed about the devil.

In England, more than they do here,
Men smoke their pipes and drink their beer;
And, at the little village inn,
Their jokes they crack, their yarns they spin,

'Til oft the last o'erflowing horn
Is drank when cocks crow in the morn;
Then for their distant homes they steer,
Rosy and hale with beef and beer.

Tom's home was near a churchyard lone,
Where back to earth went flesh and bone.
His wife would often say, "My dear,
Come home before the night draws near,

"For horrid ghosts I nightly see
Among those graves so near to me;
Just think dear Tom, what would I do
If they should run away with you?"

But Tom would laugh her fears to scorn,
And stay away till nearly morn,
Spinning his yarns with landlord Lynn
And others at the village inn.

The path that to the tavern led
Went winding by the churchyard dead;
Though wearied with the walk of miles,
Tom always leaped the churchyard stiles.

One night a crowd, with Landlord Lynn,
Assembled at the village inn;
And in the crowd the foremost one,
Was happy, brave Tom Carrington.

That night, the darkest of all nights,
They drank their beer, and told of fights
In foregin lands, and at the last,
Ghost stories came on, thick and fast.

The moments quickly speed away
Where laughs are loud and hearts are gay;
The men who to the tavern roam,
Think little of their wives at home;
The stories told among the "boys"
Are dearer than home's purest joys.

The dark clouds o'er the churchyard lower,
The old clock strikes the midnight hour;
Tom bids his jolly friends good-night,
And starts for home—a little tight.

That night an ass, by working hard,
Broke into that old lone churchyard;
And made his bed, to sleep awhile,
Across the path, close to the stile.

Tom gropes his way down lonely lane,
Across the fields, through storm and rain,
'Till lightning-flashes from the sky
Reveal the churchyard drawing nigh;

Then horrid ghosts, with fingers cold,
About whom he that night had told
Seemed rising up along the path
That led him to that yard of death.

Then all the words his wife had said
About the visits of the dead,
Came thronging in upon his brain
As fast as fell the dismal rain;

His limbs grow weak, a voice cries "run".
He shouts aloud, "Tom Carrington
What meanest thou?   Why do you quail
Before a poor old woman's tale?"

Then with a grim, courageous smile,
He lays his hand upon the stile
And makes a leap, when, O alas!
He falls astride that sleeping ass!

Up and away they swiftly go
Like arrows from the hunter's bow;
Hitting at every bound their bones
Against the white memorial stones.

If hell had opened all ablaze,
No sound from thence could match the brays
Of that poor ass, whose mighty ears,
Were wide expanded by his fears.

O'er graves long made their race they ran,
The braying ass and frightened man,
'Til with a bound the ass goes o'er
The hedge, and Tom lies at his door;
There in unconsciousness he lay
Until the dawning of the day.

*   *   *   *   *   *   *   *

No longer to the village inn
Goes Carrington, his yarns to spin;
Now, with his children on his knee,
At every eve at home is he.

The race that he and that ass ran,
Made him a better, happier man.
A hearty laugh he oft enjoys,
When thoughts of that unearthly noise
Remind him of the many boasts
He made about outwitting ghosts.

Again he laughs, to think that he,
Who boasted much of bravery,
Should through so many horrors pass,
And then be frightened by an ass.

THE FLIGHT OF THE OLD GRAY GOOSE—A FABLE.

A SCHOOL-BOY read in his reader new,
Of the wonderful things the eagles do;
How they circle around in the azure sky
Until lost to view by the naked eye,
Then fall like a flash on the helpless prey
And bear the struggling victim away
To their hungry young in the rock-bound nest
O'erhanging the foam of the ocean's breast.

The eagle he knew was a national bird—
That a patriot's heart was deeply stirred
When he saw but a gilded eagle stand
O'er the stars and stripes of his native land.

The school-boy read and pondered long
On the wonderful bird with wings so strong;
He read 'til a bright light shone in his eye,
And a wish sprang up in his boyish heart
To cage this bird of the boundless sky
And thus a small menagerie start.
Then he sighed when he thought this could not be;
For far from his home were the cliffs so grand
Where the eagle's nest hung over the sea
An hundred feet from the wave-washed sand.

A showman came to the town one day,
With all his cages in grand array;

He pitched his tent on the village green,
Which soon presented a lively scene,
The boys came out like a swarm of bees—
They covered the fences, and filled the trees;
They played at "tag" round the showman's tent
And—strange to say it—some of them went
Under the canvas and took a seat,
And sat with countenance bland and sweet,
As though they had paid a quarter or more
To enter the tent by the canvas door.

Our hero came to the village green
To see what the showman had to be seen;
He paid his money—an honest boy—
And entered the show with boundless joy.

Past cage after cage he strolled along,
From nimble monkeys to lion strong,
Until he arrived, and made a stop,
At what they had named "Curiosity Shop."
There his eyes beheld some wonderful things,
Among them a pair of eagle's wings.
A sudden desire possessed his heart
To purchase the wings ere he should depart:
And buy them he did at not a great price,
And started for home, feeling wonderful nice.

Now his good mother owned an old gray goose—
She had seen her share of the world's abuse;
For the boys from school would stone her with stones,
And the neighboring women would thrash her bones,
And cry in a rage "Of what earthly use
Is old Mother Hubbard's old gray goose!"

When John got home with his eagle's wings
He stole to the drawer and stole some strings,
And a ball of his mother's good strong yarn;
Then catching the goose near the old red barn,
He mounted the ridge and, holding tight,
He bound on the monster wings for flight.

Oh! beautiful sight that met his eyes!
Above his head were the azure skies,
And far to the westward the waters bright
Of the mill-pond fell on his gladdened sight.
"Ha! ha!" cried John, "I've an eagle now!
Thro' the waves of the azure sea she'll plow;
Now I'll see what isn't in my new book,—
A transit of Venus on my own hook."

Thus saying he swung his arms on high
To start his bird for the boundless sky;
But, oh!—alas!—with a heavy thud,
She struck below in the barn-yard mud;
And John slid down, and into the house,
With his mother's yarn, as shy as a mouse
Concluding it isn't of any use,
An eagle's an eagle—a goose, a goose.

MORAL.

If you have a son with a good strong arm—
Whom God hath fitted to till a farm—
Who loveth the fields and the sweet, fresh air
That is found in the country everywhere,
Don't say, in the pride of your heart that he
A doctor, a lawyer, or a priest shall be.

There are thousands of boys who are studying, now,
In offices dingy, with palid brow,
Who are off from the track, and should be made
To soil their hands with an honest trade:
The land is flooded with blatant quacks,
Who should be carrying peddlars' packs;
And lawyers there are who can rise no higher
Than a copying clerk near a good, warm fire;
And preachers many, are preaching today—
Not to better the world, but to block the way;
These, all, to the world, are of no more use
Than the flight from the barn of the old gray goose.

He who made the eagle with wings to soar
Far above the foam on the ocean shore,
Made, also, the smallest birds that sing
From bush to bush in the early spring;
If God, all-wise, made you not to stand
In the higher places that grace the land;
If He, in His love and wisdom, meant
That you should shine in a place below,
Toil on!—toil ever in sweet content,
And thou shall peace and happiness know.

※

HOME.

LIKE a beautiful isle, that doth peacefully smile,
    Undisturbed 'mid the wild billows' foam.
In the ocean of life, 'mid its care and its strife,
    Is the dear little haven of home.

How serene is the air, and the blossoms how fair,
  In this bright little Eden of mine;
Oh! the joys of the hearth are the purest of earth,
  And its light seemeth almost divine.

Far more precious than gold, by the miserly told;
  Far more precious than pearls from the sea—
Are the dear hearts that beat, in this blissful retreat,
  With the love that they cherish for me;
All the cares of the day quickly vanish away,
  When my feet to the threshold draw nigh;
When the dear arms entwine, and the lovely eyes shine,
  Oh, how swiftly the heart-shadows fly.

Like the ripple of brooks in the green forest nooks,
  When the storms of the winter are o'er,
Is the music so sweet of the dear little feet,
  As they patter along on the floor;
Then when cometh the night, in their raiments so white,
  The sweet cherubs bow down at my knee;
And the angels above view my Eden of love,
  And alight with a blessing for me.

Blessed spot in the sand of this lone desert land,
  Where the water-springs dance to my sight!
Blessed sheltering rock from the fierce tempest-shock!
  Brightest star of the long, weary night!
I will sing of thy charms till the death-angel's arms
  Shall reach out from the gloom of the grave;
And I go to my rest, with the loved and the blest,
  In the beautiful home o'er the wave.

THE ASS AND THE VIOLINIST—A FABLE.

WITHIN the fields, one summer day,
A storng-lunged ass began to bray;
The uplands echoed back his voice,
To hear it made his heart rejoice.

"Ah what a pity!" cried the ass,
"That I should longer feed on grass;
My lungs are strong, my voice is loud,
At concerts I might draw a crowd;
List to my music! how it fills
The valleys sleeping 'mong the hills!
'Tis sweet, I know, for, look! see what
Great ears for music I have got."

A great musician heard the din
While passing, with his violin;
He stopped awhile upon the way,
And bade the old ass cease to bray.

"My long-eared friend," the fiddler said,
"This neighborhood must wish you dead;
For, worse than any sounding brass,
Is your coarse braying, Mr. Ass;
If you wish music, cease your din,
And listen to my violin."

He rubbed the resin on his bow;
He tried the notes both high and low;
Making a stone do for a chair,
He played a grand, soul-stirring air.
Ere he had ceased his tune to play,
The ass began, again, to bray;
Nor violin, nor song of bird,
Could for a moment then be heard.

At last the old ass dropped his head
And to the old musician said:
"Music is sound, my friend, you see—
Therefore all sound must music be;
Of mine the world will be the proudest,
Because, my friend, it is the loudest."

What more could the musician say?
What further do, but let him bray?
He wandered off through twilight dim:
Ass wisdom was too much for him.

CONCLUSION.

How many men we daily pass,
Who reason like this braying ass!
They grow to men, from braggart boys,
And think that brains must make a noise;
They gain high seats in synagogues,
No mystery their vision fogs;
Whene'er they lack for argument,
They give their store of gas a vent;
And wise men whisper, when they pass,
There goes a self-conceited ass.

FIRESIDE VISIONS.

I AM toasting my toes by the bright, warm fire,
Watching the flames mounting higher and higher;
I am toasting my toes, unincumbered with shoes,
While the cares of the world seek to give me the
"blues."

I look at my home, in its humble attire,
At the darling home faces, lit up by the fire,
Then think that today, went a funeral by,
And I feel there are men who are poorer than I.

Again I look into the blaze, and I see
A vision of wealth, so amazing to me;
The lord of the mansion sits down with a grunt,
In his great habitation, with brown stone front.

Rheumatic, and gouty, he groans with his pain,
He would give all his wealth to be healthy again,
High-living now loads every breath with a sigh,
Though surrounded with gold, he is poorer than I.

The vision has gone, but another one comes
Of a gold-grasping man, with a book full of sums;
It tells of ten thousands to poor mortals lent,
Of thousands, received from his tenants, for rent.

But this man, who is on, by the gold-god enticed,
Has no love in his heart, for a crucified Christ:
As I think of his present, and future, I sigh,
And feel, there are men who are poorer than I.

Still toast I my toes, unincumbered with shoes,
But these visions have scattered the gloom of the blues;
With my hope-anchor fixed on my home in the sky,
I feel there are none who are richer than I.

FIRESIDE LONGINGS.

I AM longing again for the woods and the flowers,
   For the soft summer breezes to blow;
My heart shall rejoice when the sun-armored hours
   Shall vanquish these mountains of snow.
  I am weary of hearing the sighing and wailing
    Of winds through the leafless old trees;
I am weary of seeing the storm-clouds go sailing
    Like war-ships o'er tempest-tossed seas.

A spirit of lonliness broods o'er the mountains,
   And sighs through the valley below;
No more do I hear the sweet music of fountains,
   That sing when in summer they flow.
I am longing again for the beautiful hours
   When winter shall vanish away,
When the birds shall make nests 'mong the dew-laden
    flowers,
   And sing through the long summer day.

There are shivering ones crouched in poverty's dwelling,
   Awaiting the coming of spring;
To these, whose blue veins with the cold are now swelling,
   Winter storms can no happiness bring.
I am longing again for the beautiful hours
   When the hearts of God's numberless poor
Shall rejoice at the sight of the sunshine and showers
   Bringing plenty and warmth to their door;

When the spirit of summer shall rest on the mountains
   And laugh through the valleys below,
When the sunshine shall break the cold seal of the foun-
     tains,
   And vanquish these mountains of snow.
Then my heart shall rejoice in the beautiful hours
   When the bee and the blossom shall meet,
And I'll watch for the birth of the rainbow flowers
   In the track of the ice-king's feet.

GOOD BYE, ROBIN.

GOOD bye, pretty robin, good bye!
   I hear you are talking of leaving.
Because the cold, gray clouds are veiling the
     sky,
   And the winds drive the many-hued maple
     leaves by,
A shroud for the dead flowers weaving.

Good bye, pretty robin, good bye!
  But isn't it heaping up sorrow
To leave when the beautiful flowers all die,
And the north winds blow chilly, and mournfully sigh
  And we hope for no brighter tomorrow?

My dear little friend, can't you stay?
  You may build you a nest like the sparrows,
High up in the barn, out of everyone's way:
You may take all you wish of the clover and hay
  To shield you from winter's fierce arrows.

'Twill save you that wearisome flight,
  Your heart with your little wings throbbin';
Then, when in the spring, the sun warm and bright,
Sends the streams dancing onward like arrows of light,
  You can be, sir, the very first robin.

What, what, do you answer me no?
  Do you sigh for a home more inviting?
Where the beautiful hills wear no mantles of snow,
And the musical brooks 'neath no ice-fetters flow,
  And the sun warms the world it is lighting?

Well, dear little fellow, good bye!
  I'll welcome you back some bright morning;
Then a merry old time we will have, you and I
Adown in the meadows, where spring breezes sigh,
  And the flowers the fields are adorning.

THE DYING CHRISTIAN'S HYMN.

THOUGH life's sun is swiftly setting,
   And the valley-shades are near;
Though the angry waves are fretting,
   On the earth-shore dark and drear,
There will dawn a bright tomorrow,
   Over on the other shore;
In that land that knows no sorrow,
   I shall live forever more.

Tell me what I leave behind me,
   But a world by sin oppressed?
Earthly things each day remind me
   That this life can give no rest;
In that land that knows no sorrow,
   Over on the other shore,
When shall dawn that bright tomorrow,
   I shall rest forever more.

Farewell now to earthly pleasures,
   And the friends I love so well;
I shall gain eternal treasures,
   In the jasper citadel;
In that land that knows no sorrow,
   In that land of deathless love,
I shall claim my place tomorrow
   In the shining ranks above.

Kingly crowns are golden troubles;
    Earthly thrones are rotten things;
Worldly honors all are bubbles;
    Pleasures leave behind their stings;
In the land that knows no sorrow,
    Where no shadows ever frown,
I shall regin, a king, tomorrow,
    With my fadeless, starry crown.

PEACHES.

PEACHES are ripe, boys! Hip, hurrah!
    They hang in the moonlight rich and red;
    Ask for them, boys, don't break the law;
    Off now, off to your home and bed!
Once I was tempted—years ago—
    To take the fruit from the bending boughs;
The fellow who owned them was tight, you know,
    He always refused with lowering brows.

Ben said to me—said I to Ben
    "Let's have a taste of the old man's fruit!"
"Let's teach this stingiest man of men
    That boys can never respect a brute."
Away o'er the fences fast we sped
    Through the orchard grass, past the sleeping cows,
'Til we came to the Crawfords ripe and red
    Hanging low on the bending boughs.

Lo! there paced the old man with a frown
  Back and forth on his garden walk;
Hush, Ben, Hush! Keep down, keep down,
  The watcher will see us or hear us talk!
But Ben would giggle away in his glee,
  'Til after awhile, he laughed outright;
I think it was Ben—perhaps 'twas me—
  But, anyway, somebody laughed that night.

The old man heard it, and made a bound
For the spot by the fence where he heard the sound;
We saw him start—we started, too;
Away past the sleeping cows we flew,
On, on, with the old man close behind,
We sped, that night, like the midnight wind.

Young legs would have been too much that night
For a poor old man in his heavy flight,
Had not Ben met with a sad mishap
By falling into an unseen trap.
A woman had set her boiler down
  Just outside of her garden gate;
When Ben leaped o'er like a showman's clown
  He went right into that boiler, straight,
  Like a nickle into a collection plate.

Ben and the boiler, boiler and Ben
  Over and over and over they went;
On my side the fence there was laughter, then
  My head was down to my shoe-toes bent;
All of my strength went oozing out
  'Til I grew so weak I could hardly stand;
You guess the result, I faced about
  With my coat collar fast in the old man's hand.

Peaches are ripe, boys, hip hurrah.
  The night dews kiss 'til their cheeks are wet;
When e're I see them I feel that paw
  Pulling away on my collar, yet:
I think of the good advice he gave,
  As he led me home by the shining moon;
The old man sleeps in the silent grave,
  But I'll not forget his lesson, soon.

THE WORK OF A FARMER'S WIFE.

"THREE-FOURTHS of the women now confined
    in homes for the insane
  Are farmers' wives; 'twas overwork, and cares,
    that crazed their brain;"
  There, husband, that's what the paper says, and
    I believe 'tis true!
If my work don't let up 'fore long I shall go crazy too.

I sometimes wonder I don't fall down, and gin entirely
  out;
It's love for you and the children that keeps me stirrin'
  about;
You're away from home so much, dear John, at work in
  your out-door life,
That you don't see half of the little things that worry a
  farmer's wife.

"It's the little foxes that spoil the grapes;" it's a house-
wife's little cares
That ruffle her disposition up and give her the silver
hairs.
If, then, I'm sometimes a little cross when you come
from the fields at night,
Don't snap back, John, for remember "it always takes
two for a fight."

Just think of the work that I have to do! there is break-
fast to get in the morn
At six o'clock, so that you and the men can go to work
in the corn;
There are all the children to wash and dress, and this
must be done by rule,
For at nine o'clock the school-bell rings and they must
be off to school.

Then, when they are gone, there's the beds to make and
the rooms to sweep and dust;
There is this thing to wipe, and that thing to wipe, to
keep it from gatherin' rust;
Thus I fly around from room to room till the old farm
clock strikes ten,
And I must be gettin' dinner for a lot of hungry men.

I wonder if men-folks ever think, when they come to the
house to eat,
How hard it is to stand and cook, in the stove's, and the
summer's heat;
If they did I think they would wear a smile, instead of
an ugly frown,
When the meat is a little over-done, or the bread not
done quite brown.

When dinner is o'er, and the dishes washed, there are
    clothes to make and mend,
And, where there are children, this, you know, is a work
    that has no end;
There are little pants to cut and make; there are many
    ragged pairs
That while you, John, are sowing the wheat, keeps me a
    sewing the tares.

Soon the shadows of evening creep over woodland, hill
    and glen,
And up from the fields of waving grain, again come the
    hungry men;
Through the days of the freezing winter, and the days of
    summer heat
You men-folks, whether you work or play, are ever ready
    to eat.

I haven't mentioned the washing days, and the days
    when I stand to churn
'Till I think the butter will never come in the noisy old
    concern;
I haven't told you how hard it is to begin at mornin'
    light
And iron away on the snow-white clothes 'til the shadows
    come at night.

All this is a woman's work, dear John; 'tis the same old
    thing each day;
There is no gettin' around it, there is no runnin' away;
If women should meddle with politics the way you men
    folks do,
Creation's bottom would soon fall out, and we all go
    slidin' through.

It isn't to be wondered at that women go insane,
When love withholden starves the heart, and life's cares
    load the brain;
If husbands would speak kindly, 'twould brighten up
    her life,
And help along amazingly the work of a toiling wife.

*

GO TO BED, ROBIN, GOOD-NIGHT.

THERE, go to bed, robin, good-night!
    Save that sweet little song for the morning.
    The children now sleeping on pillows so white
    Will list to your music with greater delight,
When the morn is the cloud-land adorning.

Now, go to bed, robin, do, do!
    Come down from the twig you are swinging!
Hop into your nest 'til the night-watch is through,
Then moisten your throat with a drink of the dew,
    And finish the song you are singing.

The sun has gone down like a king;
    No longer the mill-wheels are humming;
Tuck that bright little head away under your wing,
Then while your gray nest in the night-breeze doth swing,
    You can dream of the summer days coming.

The stars are now coming out bright,
    The blue sea above you adorning;
Now go to bed, robin—good-night, good-night!
When the sun doth arise in his garment of light
    Come and tell me, sweet bird, it is morning.

HOIST BY HER OWN PETARD.

SHE was a lonely widow, in this lonely vale of
tears;
She had none to advise her, none to help her, it
appears;
But there was one thing she did have, it was plain
to old and young,
She had a fiery temper, and a most unruly tongue.

Her mansion, tho' not massive, was a solid one of brick,
In a place where such small dwellings were uncomfort-
ably thick:
'Twas in the way of progress, on a very narrow street
They had voted to make wider for the scores of tramp-
ing feet.

Like an army with its banners came the officers of law;
"That house must be demolished," that they said, and
plainly saw;
But they found before they left it it was easier to "spout"
Than to pacify the widow, and get the widow out.

As a hen flies at intruders, in protection of her chicks,
Thus she flew at the invaders walking 'round her wall of
bricks;
She robbed the dictionary of the words that burn like
fire;
They retreated in disorder from that injured woman's ire.

But the peace was only transient, like a lull amid the
    storm;
While the widow laughed and chuckled, the law was
    taking form:
The house must be demolished for the beauty of the town,
So they gave an Irishman the job, and bade him pull it
    down.

The morning dawned in glory, gilding all the city spires;
The widow, nothing dreaming, was up kindling her fires;
With their hammers and their hatchets, with their
    trowels and their squares,
The demolishers thus early took the widow unawares.

"Come out of this," said Paddy, as he hammered on the
    door.
"Never will I," then she answered, "till my blood shall
    stain the floor!"
"I'll give yees until nooning," then said he with grin
    and frown,
"If yees aint out then, my honey, I will pull your shanty
    down!"

On the grass the masons rested while the hours sped
    away,
Telling yarns, and watching closely the doomed dwelling
    old and gray;
Then, at last, the whistles sounded —then rang out the
    bells of noon,
But the widow gave no sign, or word, of moving very
    soon.

"She thinks she holds the fort, me boys," the boys said
    with a frown,
"Now mount the roof, me laddies, and take all the chim-
    neys down!"
They ran the ladder like a cat, and soon the click and
    clang
Of many a trusty trowel on the noon-day breezes rang.

The widow emptied all her beds and stuffed the stoves
    with straw;
When, lo, great clouds of inky smoke the crowds of
    gazers saw;
The masons let their trowels fall to rub their weeping
    eyes,
While straw-smoke hid the earth below, and veiled the
    very skies.

"Stand by your guns, me laddies!" the boss said with a
    shout,
She's given us the weapon now with which to put her
    out;
Then grasping sheets of iron, the chimney mouths to
    stop,
He placed them in position with an Irishman on top.

Then the tide of smoke poured downward—then the in-
    mates rubbed their eyes,
And turned their thoughts to verdant fields and the blue
    vaulted skies;
Not many moments flitted by ere the great bolts were
    drawn,
And the widow, and her kindred, gasped for breath upon
    the lawn.

Then that stubborn little woman—hoist by her own
    petard,
Found the game of fighting progress was a losing one,
    and hard;
Thus is it with us, ever, when we plan to injure men,
The dregs of every bitter cup return to us again.

IMMORTALITY.

THE flowers bloom, the flowers die;
    The winds of Autumn o'er them sigh;
    The falling leaves float sadly by.

The skies are clear at morning time
But ere the bells of evening chime,
Storm-clouds the dark horizon climb.

We smile amid our friends today—
Tomorrow, dead are we, or they;
Borne from life's active scenes away.

Is not this life? does it not seem
As though our passage was a dream?
So swiftly glide we down the stream.

And is this all for which we're made,
To walk awhile through light and shade
Like a lost sheep from pasture strayed?

Ah, no, there burns within a spark
That goes not out, though valley dark
May hide the boatman and his bark.

The soul shall live, it cannot die,
Though death's dark billow heaveth high,
And wrecks around the ferry lie!

A SONG OF HOME.

"THERE is no place like home," though 'neath
    bright skies we roam,
      In the lands where rare blossoms unfold;
      For the joys of the hearth are the purest of earth,
And its treasures more precious than gold;
How the eyes beam with love 'neath the lashes above,
    When our footsteps are heard at the door;
When we enter its bliss with a smile and a kiss,
    We feel care-worn and weary no more.

Chorus.

Shine on, hearth and home, o'er life's billows of foam,
    Oh! beautiful love-light! beautiful home!

The poor soldier in pain on the field with the slain
    And the sailor afar on the foam,
Brush the tear from the eye and look back with a sigh
    As they think of the pleasures of home:
Then in dreams of the night they again, with delight,
    Join the circle they left at the hearth,
And their hearts feel at rest, 'mid the scenes they love best
    In the sunniest spot of the earth.

The sweet nest in the wood to the lark seemeth good,
    While the eagle, with wings strong and free,
Builds her home with the flags in the towering crags
    That o'erhang the white foam of the sea.

O! it is not the spot, be it palace or cot,
　　That makes home the sweet Eden of earth,
'Tis the dear ones we meet in its blissful retreat,
　　And the love that encircles the hearth.

There are those on life's way who are homeless today,
　　And they sigh as they wearily roam;
Through the fast falling tears they look back to the years
　　That were spent in a beautiful home.
While we then are so blest with this haven of rest,
　　Let the home be made cheerful with love,
For our life is a dream,—we may soon cross the stream
　　To the beautiful mansions above.

⁂

DEATH AND CUPID.

SWEET Cupid was sleeping 'mong roses one day,
　　With his quiver of love-darts beside him,
When Death, the grim monster, came roaming that
　　way,
　　And quick with his dark eyes espied him.

"Ha! Ha!" cried the monster, "this piercer of hearts,
　　I'll play him a trick to remember;
I'll give him my arrows and take all his darts,
　　And thus turn his May to December."

So, taking the arrows, all poisoned with death,
　　He put them in Cupid's bright quiver;
Then, taking his darts, all perfumed with love's breath,
　　He left the young dreamer, forever.

When Cupid awoke from his beautiful dream,
  He peeped from his rose-perfumed dwelling,
And saw a young couple, beside a bright stream,
  Smiling sweetly, and love stories telling.

"Ah! now is my time to make one those young hearts,
  For at courting too long they have tarried;
I'll pierce them with two of my beautiful darts,
  And then they will off and get married."

So taking the arrows that Death had supplied,
  Cupid shot them with all of his power;
The youth and the maiden both sickened and died
  By the stream, in the evergreen bower.

When Death, the grim monster, left Cupid asleep,
  He saw an old man onward wending;
"Why should this poor pilgrim on earth longer weep?
  Let him go where the willows are bending."

Thus saying, Death took from his quiver a dart,
  And sped it with all of his power;
The shot was a good one; it entered his heart,
  And the old man got married that hour.

When Jupiter heard of these doings, so strange,
  A council of gods he assembled;
But none had the power the darts to exchange,
  So the world bowed with sorrow and trembled.

Since then many years have rolled rapidly by,
  Death or Cupid have never yet tarried;
The young and the beautiful sicken and die,
  The old and decrepit get married.

THE BEST COW IN PERIL.

OLD farmer B. is a stingy man,
He keeps all he gets and gets all he can;
By all his friends he is said to be
As tight as the bark on a young beach tree;
He goes to church, and he rents a pew,
But the dimes that he gives to the Lord are few;
If he gets to heaven, with the good and great,
He will be let in through the smallest gate.

Now farmer B. besides drags and plows,
Keeps a number of very fine calves and cows.
He makes no butter, but sends, by express,
The milk to the city's thirstiness.

"What do the city folks know about milk?
They are better judges of cloth and silk;
Not a man who buys, I'll vow, can tell
If I water it not, or water it well;
If they do not know, then where's the sin?
I will put the sparkling water in."
Thus talked, to himself, old farmer B.
How mean he is, young and old can see.

One night it was dark, O! fearfully dark;
The watch dog never came out to bark;
Old farmer B. in his bed did snore,
When rap! rap! rap! nearly shattered his door,

And a voice cried out with a hasty breath,
"Your best cow, neighbor, is choking to death."

Clipping off the end of a rousing snore,
Farmer B. bounded out on the bedroom floor;
And the midnight voice was heard no more·
He pulled on his pants, he knew not how,
For his thoughts were all on the choking cow;
He flew to the yards like a frightened deer,
For his stingy soul was filled with fear;
Looking all around by his lantern's light
He found that the cows were there—all right.

"I will give a dime," cried farmer B.
"To know who has played this trick on me;
May the hand be stiff, and the knuckle sore,
That knocked tonight on my farm house door."
With a scowl on his face, and a shaking head,
Farmer B. sought again his nice warm bed;
No good thoughts came, they were all o'erpowered;
The little good nature he had was soured.

When he went to water his milk next day,
That midnight voice seemed again to say,
As he pumped away with a panting breath,
"Your best cow, neighbor, is choking to death."
The meaning of this he soon found out
For *a stone was driven in the old pump's spout.*

Old farmer B. when he drives to town,
Now meets his neighbors with a savage frown;
They smile, and ask, with a kindly bow,
How getteth along the best cow, now?

IN THE OLD, FORSAKEN SCHOOL-HOUSE.

THEY'VE left the school-house, Charley, where
  years ago we sat
 And shot our paper bullets at the master's time-
  worn hat;
 The hook is gone on which it hung, and master
  sleepeth now
Where school-boy tricks can never cast a shadow o'er his
brow.

They've built a new, imposing one—the pride of all the
 town,
And laughing lads and lasses go its broad steps up and
 down;
A tower crowns its summit with a new, a monster bell,
That youthful ears, in distant homes, may hear its music
 swell.

I'm sitting in the old one, with its battered, hingeless
 door;
The windows are all broken, and the stones lie on the
 floor;
I, alone, of all the merry boys who romped and studied
 here—
Remain to see it battered up and left so lone and drear.

I'm sitting on the same old bench where we sat side by
side
And carved our names upon the desk, when not by master
eyed;
Since then a dozen boys have sought their great skill to
display,
And, like the foot-prints on the sand, our names have
passed away.

'Twas here we learned to conjugate "amo, amas, amat,"
While glances from the lasses made our hearts go pit-ti-
pat;
'Twas here we fell in love, you know, with girls who
looked us through—
Yours with her piercing eyes of black, and mine with
eyes of blue.

Our sweethearts—pretty girls were they—to us how very
dear—
Bow down your head with me, my boy, and shed for
them a tear;
With them the earthly school is out; each lovely maid
now stands
Before the one Great Master, in the house not made with
hands.

You tell me you are far out West; a lawyer, deep in
laws,
With Joe, who sat behind us here, and tickled us with
straws;
Look out for number one, my boys; may wealth come at
your touch;
But with your long, strong legal straws, don't tickle men
too much.

Here, to the right, sat Jimmy Jones—you must remember Jim—
He's teaching, now, and punishing, as master punished
  him;
What an unlucky lad he was; his sky was dark with
  woes;
Whoever did the sinning, it was Jim who got the blows.

Those days are all gone by, my boy; life's hill we're going down
With here and there a silver hair amid the school-boy
  brown;
But memory can never die, so we'll talk o'er the joys
We shared together, in this house, when you and I were
  boys.

Though ruthless hands may tear it down—this old house,
  lone and drear—
They'll not destroy the characters that started out from
  here;
Time's angry waves may sweep the shore and wash out all
  beside—
Bright as the stars that shine above—they shall for aye
  abide.

I've seen the new house, Charley; 'tis the pride of all
  the town,
And laughing lads and lasses go its broad steps up and
  down;
But you nor I, my dear old friend, can't love it half as
  well
As this condemned, forsaken one, with cracked and
  tongueless bell.

HOMEWARD BOUND.

I AM sitting by my window, watching all the passers-by;
It is evening, and the setting sun has glorified the sky,
Just as faith illumes the valley-shades when good men
  come to die.

There are passing by my dwelling, lads and lasses
  young and old,
Going home from quest of pleasure, from their graspings
  after gold;
Like the sheep that leave the pastures for the safety of
  the fold.

There's a man in costly garments; he is talking to himself,
And his fingers move uneasy, as though they handled
  pelf;
He has left the dusty counting-room, where ledgers pile
  the shelf.

His bed is in a mansion, but his rest he cannot find,
For his heart is hard and callous; he has lost his peace
  of mind
By his dealing so unjustly; by oppressions of mankind.

Poor fool! to sacrifice his all for filthy lucre's sake;
A shipwreck of his deathless soul, on barren rocks to
  make,
When the riches he is grasping through the grave he cannot take.

Now there comes the slave of fashion, she is walking prim
     and slow;
Her thoughts are written on her back, that all the world
     may know;
A dry goods exhibition, going home to close the show.

The talents God has given her are used her form to dress;
She passes by, with haughty head, the poor in their dis-
     tress;
The Lord of Light will pass by her, when He the good
     shall bless.

She has no share in purer joys, that spring from doing
     good,
Like flowers to cheer man's rugged path, through life's
     dim-lighted wood;
The joys that, where they light the heart, their worth is
     understood.

Here come the workmen from the shops, who lead a toil-
     ing life;
'Tis evening that has called them, from the bustle and
     the strife,
To the home where rest awaits them, to the babes and
     loving wife.

They glory not in ancestry; they boast not of their birth;
A toiling hand, an honest heart, they count of greater
     worth:
No dimes are in their pockets, wrung from needy ones of
     earth.

Pass on, brave toilers, to your homes! in overalls of
    blue;
The world is what it is, today, because of such as you.
Yours is the rest of honor when the day of toil is
    through.

Ah! there he comes, a poor old man; his steps are feeble
    now;
The gray hairs hang adown his neck, and hide his wrin-
    kled brow;
Three score and ten, with all their cares, have made the
    strong man bow.

He goeth down the steps of life, how swift the years do
    glide!
He soon will enter two bright homes, where loving ones
    abide,
The humble one across the street—the one across the tide.

I am sitting by my window, but I see no passers-by;
It is night now, and the shining stars are looking from
    the sky,
Bright windows to that better home where mortals never
    die.

Dear home, beyond the flight of time, where nothing
    shall molest,
The chart of God, shall guide my bark safe o'er the
    foaming crest,
'Til I joyfully drop ancnor in the quiet of thy rest.

THE OLD, AND THE NEW YEAR.

SOFTLY! softly! silently tread!
For the New Year is born, and the old year is
    dead;
Its days are all numbered; its moments are fled.

Every year, when we reach this lone spot in the stream,
We, all, with one breath, pronounce life but a dream;
So near doth the Judge and eternity seem.

Every year, resolutions like vapor arise,
And our rainbows of promise we weave in the skies;
But how soon—Ah! how soon—all their loveliness dies.

In the year that has gone 'neath life's turbulent wave,
Silver hairs have stole in, though the heart has been brave,
Silver heads gone down to the rest of the grave.

In the year Time has borne to the tomb of the Past,
There were bright, sunny spots; but the stream ran so fast
The flukes would not catch, though the anchor was cast.

There were bright, sunny days; there were dismal ones too;
In the depths of great sorrows a hand led us through,
'Til the morn-light of happiness broke to our view.

The new year is with us; the old year is dead;
Let us sieze on the moments before they are fled;
Let us press to the goal that is shining ahead.

Lend a hand to thy brother who falls by the way!
Give a word of advice to the tempted who stray!
That the Angel of Peace in thy dwelling may stay.

FIELD AND WAYSIDE FLOWERS.

I'VE seen wild flowers so wondrous fair,
   So beauteous to behold,
That, if the plants had been more rare,
   Their worth would be untold·
But, blossoming on every hill,
   'Neath bright or cloudy sky,
They did not with their beauty thrill
   The common passer-by.

But, should the time come rolling round,
   When, by the paths we plod,
These well known plants no more are found
   Decking the meadow's sod,
We then shall miss the the beauteous flowers,
   And wish them here once more,
To gladden through the summer hours,
   The field, the wood, the shore.

'Tis thus with many blessings bright,
   That God on us bestows;
They comfort us from morn till night,
   From year's birth to its close,
And not until they flee from earth,
   And we in sadness roam,
Do we appreciate the worth
   Of health, and friends, and home.

BY AND BY.

WE'LL all be through by and by,
　　With the hurry and worry for gold;
　　When the light shall fade from the spark·
　　　　ling eye,
And we sit at eve with the day gone by
And the shadows of night enfold.

We'll all be through by and by,
　　With loving the things that fade;
For we must perish and lowly lie
Where the willows bend and the night winds sigh,
　　In our home by the sexton made.

We'll all be through by and by
　　With the sorrows that crowd our way,
The storms that sweep o'er the heart's dark sky
Will cease, and a peace will come by and by
　　With the dawn of a brighter day.

We'll all be through by and by
　　With the friend and the bitterest foe;
And side by side we'll peacefully lie
Where the grasses fade and the flowers die,
　　And the mourners come and go.

Then watch with a mariner's eye
　　For the beautiful land so near;
Tho' the night be dark and the waves run high,
Through the gloom ahead we shall soon descry
　　The lights on eternity's pier.

HYMNS.

FAITH IS THE VICTORY.*

"The victory that overcometh the world, even our faith.—1 John 5: 4.

ENCAMPED along the hills of light,
  Ye Christian soldiers, rise,
  And press the battle ere the night
  Shall veil the glowing skies;
Against the foe in vales below,
Let all our strength be hurled;
Faith is the victory, we know,
  That overcomes the world.

His banner over us is love,
  Our sword the word of God;
We tread the road the saints above
  With shouts of triumphs trod;
By faith they, like a whirlwind's breath,
  Swept on o'er ev'ry field;
The faith by which they conquered Death
  Is still our shining shield.

On ev'ry hand the foe we find
  Drawn up in dread array;
Let tents of ease be left behind,
  And onward to the fray;

*By permission of Bigelow & Main Company

Salvation's helmet on each head
    With truth all girt about,
The earth shall tremble 'neath our tread,
    And echo with our shout.

To him that overcomes the foe,
    White raiment shall be giv'n
Before the angels he shall know
    His name confessed in heaven;
Then onward from the hills of light,
    Our hearts with love aflame;
We'll vanquish all the hosts of night,
    In Jesus' conquering name.

OUR NAMES IN HEAVEN.*

REJOICE, rejoice, O child of light,
    Unknown to earthly fame;
    Far, far beyond these scenes of night
    Shines forth your humble name;
    By angel hand, at God's command
With joy 'twas written down;
On that blest day you sought the way
    To win a fadeless crown.

Rejoice, rejoice, ye homeless saints,
    Who own no mansion here;
Forever cease your sad complaints,
    And dry each falling tear;

*By permission of Bigelow & Main Company.

Far, far away, in endless day,
　Where dwell the good and true,
A mansion stands, not made with hands,
　All fitted up for you.

Rejoice, rejoice, ye weary ones,
　Who long with cares have striv'n,
For brighter far than many suns
　Shines forth your name in heav'n;
To that fair shore shall come no more
　The ills we suffer here;
Those regions blest give perfect rest,
　And life without a tear.

Then let us cease to envy those
　Who gain earth's pomp and pow'r;
Their glory, like the fading rose,
　Is only for an hour;
But we shall live where God doth give
　Eternal life and love;
Within the gate our dear ones wait,
　To welcome us above.

THE BEAUTIFUL HILLS.*

Who shall ascend into the hill of the Lord?—Ps.
XXIV—3.

O, THE Beautiful Hills of the By-and-By!
　By faith I can trace their forms,
As they rest in the glow of that fadeless sky
　Unswept by earth's chilling storms;

*By permission of Bigelow & Main Company.

There the river of life floweth on so bright,
  The Beautiful Hills between,
And the saints all in white, with their crowns of light,
  On the evergreen shores are seen.

Chorus.

O, the hills, the hills, the Beautiful Hills,
  Where the feet of the ransomed tread!
May I breathe the perfume in that land of bloom
  When life with its cares has fled.

On the Beautiful Hills of the By-and-By!
  Are friends I have loved so long;
And at times it doth seem they are hov'ring nigh
  To sing their redemption song:
Then my love flames anew, and my hopes grow bright,
  And joy all my being thrills,
And I journey along through earth's weary night,
  In the light from the Beautiful Hills.

O, the Beautiful Hills of the By-and-By!
  No valleys of death between:
It is there that no tear ever dims the eye
  That feasts on each rapt'rous scene:
O, they need not the sun in that blissful clime!
  The Lamb with his glory fills
All the mansions so fair, and the city sublime
  On the Beautiful, Beautiful Hills.

THE HARBOR BELL.*

"We were nearing a dangerous cost, and night was drawing near, suddenly a heavy fog setteled down upon us; no lights were sighted, the pilot seemed anxious and troubled, not knowing how soon we might be dashed to pieces on the hidden rocks along the shore.

The whistle was blown loud and long, but no response was heard; the Captain ordered the engines to be stopped and for some time we drifted about on the waves; suddenly the pilot cried—Hark ! and far away in the distance, we heard the welcome tones of the Harbor Bell, which seemed to say, this way,—this way. Again the engines were started, and guided by the welcome sound we entered the port in safety."

OUR life is like a stormy sea,
    Swept by the gales of sin and grief,
    While on the windward and the lee
    Hang heavy clouds of unbelief;
But o'er the deep a call we hear,
    Like harbor bell's inviting voice;
It tells the lost that hope is near,
    And bids the trembling soul rejoice.

O let us now the call obey,
    And steer our bark for yonder shore,
Where still that voice directs the way,
    In pleading tones for evermore;
A thousand life wrecks strew the sea;
    They're going down at ev'ry swell;
"Come unto me," "Come unto me,"
    Rings out th' inviting harbor bell.

*By permission of Bigelow & Main Co.

O tempted one, look up, be strong;
   The promise of the Lord is sure,
That they shall sing the victor's song,
   Who faithful to the end endure;
God's Holy Spirit comes to thee,
   Of His abiding love to tell;
To blissful port, o'er stormy sea,
   Calls heav'ns assuring harbor bell.

Come, gracious Lord and, in thy love,
   Conduct us o'er life's stormy wave;
O guide us to the home above,
   The blissful home beyond the grave;
There safe from rock, and storm, and flood,
   Our song of praise shall never cease,
To Him who bought us with His blood,
   And brought us to the port of peace.

Chorus.

This way, this way, O heart oppress'd
   So long by storm and tempest driv'n;
This way, this way, lo, here is rest,
   Rings out the harbor bells of heaven.

THE GLORIOUS CHURCH.*

A glorious Church—Eph. 5: 27.

O CHURCH of Christ, divinely fair,
   March on to victory!
No jewels can with thee compare,
   From richest mine or sea;

When drifting on in sins dark night,
  Amid the tempest's strife,
I saw thy glorious beacon light,
  And found the way of life.

Chorus.

O glorious church, shine out, shine out,
  O'er rock, and shoal and wave!
O watchman still the message shout,
  Christ can the sinful save.

O Church of Christ, my safety tower,
  I to thy shelter fled,
When fiery darts, by Satan's power,
  Were flying thick o'erhead,
Nor will I from my refuge go,
  Though by the world enticed:
No other doctrines will I know
  Than Thine, O Church of Christ!

O Church of Christ, thy fellowship
  Can sweeter pleasure bring
Than nectar which the worldlings sip,
  At banquets of the king!
For lasting joy and peace of mind
  In sin we vainly search;
There are no joys like those I find
  In Jesus and his church.

O glorious church, I'll sing of thee
  Until life's latest hour!
Thy worship shall my pleasure be,
  Thy faith and love my power:

Thy songs of praise shall still inspire
My soul to deeds of love,
Until I join the Heavenly choir
In sweeter songs above.

&

THE MANSION OF LIGHT.*

O THE mansions of light, blissful mansions of light'
We are coming their glory to see;
We are coming thro' tempest, thro' sorrow and
night,
With the King in His beauty to be.

Chorus.

For we know if this house we inhabit today
Were dissolved in the depths of the tomb,
We've a building of God, in that land far away,
Where the Spring-time forever shall bloom.

There no night spreads its mantle o'er valleys and hills,
Hiding beauties and glories untold;
There no winter shall silence the song of the rills,
And the dwellers shall never grow old.

Yet a little while here—for the wings of the years
Speed us on to that far away shore—
Then away we shall fly from this valley of tears
To the land where they sorrow no more

*By permission of Bigelow & Main Company.

THE WANDERING BOY.

I HEARD the close of his dwelling door,
   The latch of the old homegate,
And I know that a boy has gone forth once
      more
To the paths where the tempters wait;
Has gone like a bird to the fowler's snare;
And soon, ah soon, he may perish there.

Chorus.

O save the boy, the wandering boy,
   From perilous sins of youth!
O turn his feet to the save retreat,
   Of purity, love and truth.

Allured away by a phantom light,
   And charmed by a siren's song,
He's drifting out to a darker night,
   Where the fetters of sin are strong;
Ere lost to his home, to all hope and joy,
   Oh who will save the wandering boy?

A mother sits in her old arm chair,
   And weeps by the dim fire light;
She pleads with God in an anxious prayer
   For her boy once so pure and bright;
She weeps and she waits until late—so late,
   To hear the latch of the old home gate.

Come in, O wandering boy, come in!
The clouds gather dark o'er head;
The snare is there, in your path of sin,
And the thorns where your feet now tread;
Come in, O come in, like a tired dove,
The ark is here, and God is love.

O CHRISTIAN, SPEED THEE.*

O CHRISTIAN, speed thee on thy way,
Lay every burden down;
For thee the King doth now display,
In realms of everlasting day,
A never fading crown.

Chorus.

Then speed away! then speed away!
Lay every burden down,
O look not back, but onward press,
And gain the promised crown.

Forget the things which are behind—
The sins and follies past;
Increasing strength thy soul shall find;
Then onward, onward like the wind,
And to the course hold fast.

*By permission of Bigelow & Main Company.

A cloud of witnesses behold
   Thy progress in the way;
Press on! thy triumph shall be told
By angel choirs with harps of gold,
   When comes the crowning day.

On Jesus fix thy longing eyes;
   The Author of thy faith
Shall help thee win the glorious prize,
And bid thee welcome to the skies,
   When fall the shades of death.

         *

ROOM FOR JESUS,*

HAST thou no room within thy heart,
   Where Jesus may abide?
And canst thou say to Him, "Depart,"
   Who for thee bled and died?

No room for Him whose glory light,
   In lowly manger laid,
Shone forth in heav'nly mansions bright
   Before the worlds were made!

I will, O Lord unbar the door;
   No longer stand outside
But come within, and evermore
   In my poor heart abide.

Abide with me, thro' all my days,
   Thy presence be my light;
Then shall my mouth show forth Thy praise,
   And I shall walk aright.

*By permission of Bigelow & Main Company.

When comes at last the judgment day,
  And I Thy face shall see,
What joy supreme to hear **Thee** say,
  "Come in, there's room for thee."

Chorus.

O yes, there's room within my heart,
  There's room, O Lord, for Thee;
Come in and never more depart;
  Come in; abide with me.

PRAY FOR ME.*

PRAY for me, I need your prayers,
  When before the throne you bow:
  With my sins, and doubts, and cares,
  I would come to Jesus now:
  Pray for me, that peace be given,—
God's sweet peace, a boundless sea;—
Then His love shall be my heaven;
  Christians, will you pray for me?

Chorus.

Pray for me, I need your prayers;
  Weak I feel myself to be;
To the cross, with doubts and cares
  I am coming—pray for me.

Pray for me, that I may live
  Near the cross of Calvary:
That my lamp more light may give,
  Christians, will you pray for me?

*By permission of Bigelow & Main Company.

Pray for me, that when in pain,
I may suffer patiently,
And not murmur or complain,
Though the night seem long to me.

Pray for me, that I may wear
God's whole armor constantly;
And be faithful everywhere:
Christians, will you pray for me?
Pray for me, that when, at last,
I shall lay my armor down,
Trials o'er, and warfare past,
I may wear the victor's crown.

DAY BY DAY.*

GLADLY I have walked with Jesus,
Through the bright and joyous day
While the warm and glowing sunshine
Cheered me on my pilgrim way;
Flowers were blooming, birds were singing
Sweetly over vale and hill,
But the precious love of Jesus
Made the world seem brighter still.

Day by day I'll follow Jesus,
Day by day, what e're may come,
Knowing well his hand so tender
Leads me safely, safely home.

*By permission of Bigelow & Main Company.

Safely I have walked with Jesus,
  Through the darkest shades of night,
While the tempest raged around me,
  Not a glimmering star in sight;
Thorns were piercing, hope seemed dying
  'Neath the cruel tempter's power;
But the precious love of Jesus
  Kept me safely every hour.

By and by I'll walk with Jesus,
  In the blissful realms of light
And behold the saved and ransomed
  All arrayed in spotless white;
There I'll join the joyful singing
  Of that glad triumphant throng
Where the precious love of Jesus
  Shall forever be my song.

❧

WHERE JESUS OF NAZARETH DWELLS.

Master, where dwellest thou?   And he saith unto them
come and see.

O COME weary sinner, all laden with guilt,
  Thou mayest have pardon and peace if thou wilt!
  Thy doubts may be banished, thy wounds be made
      whole
And the joy of the Lord may illumine thy soul:
Why carry thy burdens ?   Why fear thou the grave,
When one who is mighty, is willing to save ?
O hear the old story God's word freely tells,
Come, see where this Jesus of Nazareth dwells!

Chorus.

Come and see for thyself, come and see, come and see,
What Jesus thy Savior has purchased for thee!
The mountains of joy and the peace-breathing dells
Of the Kingdom where Jesus of Nazareth dwells.

The voice of thy mother in infancy's days,
Sang softly of Jesus, his love and his praise;
Perhaps she has gone to the mansions above
To know more and more of his infinite love:
Knowest thou how she prayed—how in secret she wept—
That you might from sin and temptation be kept ?
O heed, then, the story the Spirit now tells,
Come, see where this Jesus of Nazareth dwells.

The word of the Lord is a lamp for thy feet;
Its warnings are truthful, its counsels are sweet:
Why cover its rays with thy blind unbelief,
And walk in the dark road of burdens and grief ?
The preachers of righteousness, day after day,
Have told thee of Jesus, and pointed the way;
Their words, and the voice of the church-going bells,
Invite thee where Jesus of Nazareth dwells.

O quench not the Spirit by longer delay!
This constant refusing may grieve him away,
And thou shalt be left to thy self and thy sins,
Till the reapers go forth and the harvest begins:
If God's Holy Spirit should from thee depart,
And leave thee alone to thy hardness of heart,
Nor preacher, nor bible, nor church-going bells,
Can bring thee where Jesus of Nazareth dwells.

THEY SHALL SHINE AS THE STARS.

THRICE blessed are they, who by counsel or song,
Turn men to the right from the thraldom of
wrong:
More blessed than Kings with their crowns of pure
gold,
Bestudded with diamonds, of value untold:
For Kingdoms shall crumble, and thrones shall decay,
And the glory of nations shall vanish away,
But they who turn men to the love-life divine,
Like the bright stars of even forever shall shine.

Chorus.

They shall shine as the stars! They shall shine as the
stars!
Far greater than heroes from holiest wars,
They shall shine as the stars —shall eternally shine—
Who turn men from sin to the love-life divine!

Go, then, to the highways and hedges of sin!
Tell men of the great feast, and welcome them in!
Tell them that for sinners the table is spread—
That all that will come shall be bountifully fed:
Go, beacon the darkness that covers the foam,
And guide with your bright light the perishing home!
For those who turn men to the love-life divine
Like the bright stars of even forever shall shine.

Do not, then, grow weary, nor faint by the way!
Well doing shall reap at the great harvest day!
Shall reap the eternal and blessed reward,—
The welcome "well done" and the smile of the Lord:
When empires have crumble and thrones have decayed,
And kings are no more who the scepter have swayed,
When the touch of the Lord shall the mountains have
    rent
Ye shall shine as the stars of the bright firmament.

❦

COMING, PRESCIOUS SAVIOUR.*

WE are coming, precious Saviour, in the fervor
    of our youth,
    Gladly coming to Thy service, in the cause of
    love and truth;
    We are singing, ever singing of the Cross of
    Calvary,
While we earnestly endeavor, day by day, to follow Thee.

Lead us safely, Tender Shepherd, to the waters cool and
    bright;
In Thy fold provide us shelter, when shall fall the shades
    of night
When the way is rough and thorny, or when blows the
    chilling blast,
Bear us safely in Thy bosom, till the danger all is past.

---

*By permission of Bigelow & Main Company.

Do Thou guide us, blessed Master, in the way that we
   should go:
As the fleeting years go by us, may the pathway brighter
   grow
'Till the way shall end in glory, where the crowns of life
   are given,
Where we'll praise Thee, blest Redeemer, in the perfect
   bliss of heav'n.

Chorus.

We are marching, onward marching, a united Junior
   band;
And we'll sound Thy praise, O Saviour, over all our favored land.

WITHOUT THEE, MY SAVIOUR *

"Without me ye can do nothing."—Jesus.

WITHOUT thee, my Saviour, I nothing can do.
I strive, but I fail to be faithful and true:
My strength is all weakness, and faint is my
      heart,
   Unless thou art nigh me thy grace to impart.

Chorus.

Abide with me ever, O Saviour abide,
My refuge in danger, in darkness my guide.

Without thee, my Saviour, I struggle in vain;
I sink 'neath the wave with no arm to sustain;
But when thou art with me to strengthen my soul,
I cling to the rock though the waves o'er me roll.

*By permission of Bigelow & Main Company.

Without thee, my Saviour, I cannot prevail
When foes of my soul with their weapons assail:
But when thou art with me to gird me with might,
I march to the battle and win in the fight.

Without thee, my Saviour, I soon go astray
Where thorns pierce my feet and where night hides my
    way;
But with thee to guide me my pathway doth lead
Through pastures so green, where thy flocks safely feed.

O, then, be thou ever the guide of my life—
My rock in the tempest, my shield in the strife—
My counsellor here as I journeyed alone,
My righteousness there, when I stand at thy throne.

                        ❧

HAVE FAITH IN GOD.*

Air—"Abide With Me."

LIFT up thy head, O thou desponding one!
    Have faith in God and wipe away thy tears:
    Behind the clouds still brightly shines the sun,
    And God is love through all the passing years·

Have faith in God, the darkest day is fraught
    With some great blessing hidden in disguise;
The human heart in sorrow must be taught
    Some lessons meant to fit it for the skies.

*By permission of Bigelow & Main.

Have faith in God, and bravely breast the tide;
　　The light will dawn, though darkness may increase:
Then they who trustingly in God abide
　　Shall find sweet rest and sing their hymn of peace.

And when, at last, we see His face above,
　　We shall forever know as we are known:
Ah, then, we'll find that all God's ways were love,
　　And praise and wonder 'round His glorious throne.

⚜

THE PEARL OF THE CROSS.

"The Kingdom of heaven is like unto a merchant man
seeking goodly pearls; who, when he had found one pearl
of great price, went and sold all that he had and bought
it."—Matt. 13th, 45-46.

A MERCHANT man sought 'neath the skies so fair,
The beautiful pearls that the wild waves bear;
He sought till he found it, one gem alone,
The pearl of all pearls that the world had known:
　He parted with all for the beautiful gem,
And soon it was set in the King's diadem.

I know of a pearl that is richer, far,
Than all of the gems of the ocean are;
I sought and I found it with joyful heart
And never will I with my treasure part:
When life with its pleasures doth seek to entice,
Still firmer I cling to my pearl of great price.

The pearl of all pearls to this dark world given
Is Jesus, the glory and joy of heaven;
The wise men of old found the precious gem
Laid low in the manger at Bethlehem,
And millions today count the world to be loss
For Jesus, the Saviour, the Pearl of the Cross.

O come weary sinner, by guilt oppressed,
For you there is pardon, and peace and rest;
For Jesus has shed his most precious blood
To bring thy poor wandering soul to God:
O love not the world with its glitter and gloss,
But seek ye the Saviour, the Pearl of the Cross.

Then shalt thou rejoice with a joy unknown,
And angels shall echo it 'round the throne,
And sing till the mansions above resound
"The dead is alive and the lost is found!"
Then come weary sinner, count all things but dross
For Jesus, the Saviour, the Pearl of the Cross.

❧

O, FOR A DEEPER WORK OF GRACE.

"Thou shalt be near me."—Gen. XLV—10.

O FOR a deeper work of grace,
    A closer walk, O Lord, with thee:
    A brighter view of thy dear face
      Beaming with peace and love on me.

*By permission of Bigelow & Main Company.

Chorus.

Closer, closer, draw me closer,
  Closer to thy bleeding side:
Nearer, dearer, skies grown clearer
  Let me 'neath thy wings abide.

O guide me to a deeper sea,
  Where shoals of doubt are all unknown:
Where thou art all in all to me,
  And my poor heart is thine alone.

Before the mercy seat I bow;
  No longer would I walk by sight;
O fill me with thy fullness, now,
  And bid me journey in the light.

So shall my life be full of love,
  My lamp refilled shall brightly shine
Until I see thy face above
  And bear an image, Lord, like thine.